THE DIGITAL SILK ROAD

CHINA'S STEALTH INVASION OF EUROPE

by

CHRIS KNOWLES

Chris Knowles

The Digital Silk Road

Chris Knowles

The Digital Silk Road

ALSO BY CHRIS KNOWLES

Murder in Martha's Vineyard Lodge: A Masonic Allegory

Murder in Sugarbush Lodge: A Study in Brotherhood

Murder in Georgetown Lodge: Prelude to Armageddon

A Matter of Perception

The Cambridge Incident

*The Head of the Snake: The ISIS Assault on
Martha's Vineyard*

An Ill Wind from the East

Upon This Rock

War at the Top of the World: The Battle for the Arctic Shelf

*The Disciples in Times Square:
The ISIS Showdown at the Crossroads of the World*

The Falklands Gambit

*The Eagle, The Bear and The Dragon:
The Zumwalt's Final Trial*

Chris Knowles

The Strait of Gibraltar

Shadow Government

*Patriots on the Watchtower: The Second
American Revolution*

Kessel Run: The Digital Battlefield

The Polar Silk Road: China's Arctic Ambush

Hiroshima Redux: North Korea's Breakout

Skipping Stones: The Oil War of the Hypersonics

*Peace is at Hand:
From the Cuban Missile Crisis
to Operation Linebacker*

Two Chinas: Reining in the Rogue

Chapter One

During the first half of the Twentieth Century, if one were to ask an American what the phrase "political geography" meant to them, they would most likely conjure up an image of the outline of a white continent with oceans on either side. Within the outline of that continent would be black lines representing the borders of the 48 contiguous states. After 1959 there would have been small insets in the upper and lower left-hand corners with out-of-scale outlines of Alaska and Hawaii.

However, in the politically-supercharged Twenty-first Century shading within the borders of each state would have idiosyncratically taken on red, blue, and sometimes even purple hues representing states from which the majority of electoral votes in the most recent presidential election had gone to the Republican or Democrat candidate respectively or for which there was a trend from one party to the other. The states along the Atlantic and Pacific coasts would be overwhelmingly blue while in the middle, with some notable exceptions, would be the predominantly red states which are derogatorily referred to in the media as "flyover country". We have *The New York Times* to blame for this, and thank heaven for color television, *USA Today*, and the internet.

Moving from the "macro" level one step down, if looked at at the county level, most states would appear to be predominantly red in their rural counties and blue in the urban areas. This leads to several states wherein the state legislature, whose representatives are chosen by county or district, are from one party but the governor, who is chosen by statewide vote, is from the other.

In 2021 there were counties and groups of counties that are taking steps to secede from the rest of their state or become part of an adjoining state with a more similar political bent. Taken one step further, if broken down by zip codes, the wealthier ones would usually be red while the poorer would be blue. At the neighborhood level, the same would hold true. Taken at the ward, or city block, level and stepping out of politics and into the realm of urban violence, political geography could equally well capture a predominant gang's spread throughout a public housing project during the course of its inevitably deadly turf wars.

In its simplest terms, political geography is the study of the movement of political phenomena across space over time.

In Europe, when maps of its countries come to mind they are frequently shaded or grouped using a couple of vastly different criteria. Following World War II in 1949 the North Atlantic Treaty Organization (NATO) was formed which created a mutual defense alliance predominantly among the democracies and monarchies as well as Canada and the United States, one of the world's two superpowers.

Their counterparts to the East were the Warsaw Pact countries which consisted of the Soviet Union, the other superpower, and seven other "Eastern Bloc" socialist republics.

Although NATO still exists, the Warsaw Pact alliance was dissolved in February of 1991 and its most powerful member, the Soviet Union, itself ceased to exist in December of that same year. However, a new confederation of 28 states (27 following the exit by the United Kingdom under BREXIT in 2020) came into being in 1993 under the terms of the Maastricht Treaty; the European Union with its accompanying concept of European citizenship.

While in Europe one of the political and economic phenomena which can be tracked from the East moving West is socialism, the easiest and most remarkable is Communism. If we were to start with the October Revolution of 1917 in Saint Petersburg, Russia, we would find a trend showing the Westward spread of a European brand of Communism referred to as Eurocommunism which did not definitively conclude until the 1980s. The distinctions between Communism and Eurocommunism were the degree of allegiance and subservience to the Soviet Union and those were widely severed following the putting down of the Czechoslovakian revolution in 1968 by the Soviet Union.

Referred to as the "Prague Spring", it was precipitated

by Romanian Nicolae Ceauşescu's speech in which he adamantly criticized the Soviet invasion of Czechoslovakia and expressed his support for Czech leader Alexander Dubček. Although the Portuguese Communist Party (PCP) supported the Soviets, the Italian Communist Party (PCI) and the Communist Party of Spain (PCE) dissented. The Communist Party of France (PCF) condemned the Soviet occupation. The PCF had advocated for a cessation of hostilities but disapproved of the Soviet intervention, a first for a Western European Communist party in directly and openly criticizing Soviet policy.

In scanning the numerous Communist parties in Europe, one of the most dominant nations is missing; Germany. In post-World War II Europe they held a unique position. Under the terms of the peace treaty which brought the war to a conclusion, Germany was divided into the German Democratic Republic (GDR), East Germany, which was occupied and administered by the Soviet Union, and the Federal Republic of Germany, known as West Germany, whose three zones were administered by the United States, the United Kingdom, and France. Those wishing to live under Communism could simply stay in, or relocate to, East Germany. However, those who found themselves living in East Germany who did not want to live under Communism were not permitted by the Soviet Union to leave.

The oldest Communist organization among the major countries in Western Europe was the Communist Party of

Great Britain (CPGB) founded in July 1920. Formal party organization had leapt across half the continent and spanned the English Channel. Communism was attractive to many in the trade unions and other workers' groups. But, as working conditions improved, the core of the party shifted to the students and professors in academia and other intellectual segments of society. It was from these groups that many Cold War-era Communist spies were recruited to be infiltrated throughout the United States. Following the collapse of the Soviet Union, the party dissolved in 1991.

The next party to be formed was the Communist Party of France (PCF) in December of the same year. Its membership came from the socialist French Section of the Workers' International Party. Ho Chi Minh, the leader of the North Vietnamese independence movement, was one of its leaders. The party was banned as a result of the German – Soviet Non-aggression Pact due to its membership in the Soviet Communist International, or Comintern, which opposed the Second World War.

Before Germany invaded the Soviet Union the following year, in 1941 the PCF formed the National Front, a faction within the French *Resistance*. Simultaneously, the PCF began to collaborate with Charles de Gaulle's "Free France" government in exile and took part in the National Council of the Resistance (CNR). By the end of the German occupation of France in 1944, the party had gained great acceptance in many parts of France. It still exists today.

In 1921 the Italian (PCI), Portuguese (PCP), and Spanish (PCE) Communist parties were formed. In Italy, dictator Mussolini outlawed the PCI in 1926. It regained its formal legal status in 1943. It was dissolved in 1991. The PCP was declared illegal in 1926 and remained so until 1929. Although it had been outlawed during the Fascist regime, in 1943 the PCI became the second largest political party in Italy after the war. It garnered a third of the vote in the 1970s. The PCP remains to this day. The PCE was the principal opposition to the dictatorship of Generalissimo Francisco Franco. As with the PCP, the PCE persists.

The creation of the European Union (EU) in 1993 was the first subtle step in a movement toward a society that would be susceptible to the tenets of Communism. Universal citizenship made citizens of each member state feel as though they were part of a greater whole. The ability to cross national boundaries with one universal passport was both liberating and invigorating. And the existence of a single monetary system with a single universal currency, the Euro, made the residents believe that their money would always be good. That concept had not always held true in pre-EU Europe.

The circumstances had been established for the creation of one mutually-supportive society. But this time the thrust was not being derived from Moscow. This time the structure and security would be emanating from Beijing.

Chapter Two

From the days of Chinese dynasties which predated the birth of Christ by over two millennia until today's Communist Party of China (CPC), the Chinese have always adhered to a belief that it was their destiny, if not their right, to rule the world. Their behavior had frequently belied that belief. And now the CPC was convinced that their nation possessed the intellect and power to make that belief a reality.

But China had frequently approached their crusades in a none-too-subtle manner. By casting themselves as the aggressor or adversary, they had tipped their hand. But by the 2020s President Xi Jinping and the CPC had mastered the art of finesse. They did not begin an initiative as a foe but rather as an ally. The key to getting another regime on board with a plan which would ultimately benefit China was to ensure the other nation that the venture would benefit them in the short run.

In modern times, trade between China and Europe has most frequently followed the sea route which has been referred to as the "One Road". Starting on China's Pacific coast, ships would sail South through the South China Sea and then Northwest through the Strait of Malacca to either Southeastern India or the island nation now known as Sri Lanka at the Southern tip of the Indian subcontinent.

From there the ships would sail West across the Arabian Sea to the Somali coast and then follow the African coastline through the Gulf of Aden and the Red Sea to the Suez Canal. Only after passing through the canal would they gain access to the Southern European coast. Traversing the Mediterranean and the Strait of Gibraltar would gain them ports in Northern Europe and the British Isles.

In 2013, the Chinese government first began to explore the possibility of restoring the terrestrial path once called the Silk Road and now renamed "One Belt". The "One Belt, One Road" initiative, or OBOR, was meant to create rail connections from China across Asia to carry Chinese goods to Istanbul where they would pick up a choice of refurbished railway paths vaguely resembling the old routes of the Orient Express through Southern and Western Europe to Paris. If they so desired, they could even use the "Chunnel" to deliver goods to the center of London itself. Thus, China would have its choice of sea or land routes to transport their goods to the lucrative European markets. The One Belt would supplement the trade which followed the One Road.

On March 28, 2015, the CPC released a white paper outlining the parameters of the Belt and Road Initiative (BRI). It was issued by the National Development and Reform Commission (NDRC), the Ministry of Foreign Affairs (MOFA), and the Ministry of Commerce

(MOFCOMM) of the People's Republic of China (PRC). However, buried in the white paper were provisions for the aggressive export of digital technologies.

In what one could only imagine was a humanitarian gesture, China was going to make a significant investment in African nations in order to bring their development fully into the Twenty-first Century. That investment was to be made in the form of introducing numerous applications of digital technology. By 2020, the PRC had entered into agreements or memoranda of understanding with at least sixteen African countries. "At least" because some relationships may remain unacknowledged or not uncovered. China was providing more subsidies for information technology than all of the multinational organizations and leading Western governmental agencies combined.

But the governments in many of the recipient nations were using Chinese technology, software, and hardware to prop up and secure their repressive regimes. Huawei and ZTE among others were providing their high-tech wares to support surveillance networks and censorship tools while supplying advanced social media monitoring techniques to allow governments to locate and rout out subversive groups or others who were trying to undermine the existing repressive power structure.

Huawei, for example, was marketing what is referred to as a "Safe City" program in Botswana, Ghana, the Ivory

Coast, Kenya, Mauritius, Morocco, South Africa, Uganda, Zambia, and Zimbabwe. This was accompanied by Cloudwalk's mass surveillance facial recognition program which allowed for the monitoring of the movements of suspected dissidents. And the computer software and hardware which provided for the implementation of these projects could review the endless and multitudinous volumes of incoming data at rates that were faster than humans' by unimaginably large factors of 10.

The exports which China is either marketing or distributing to African nations include telecom network cables, digital partnerships with universities, surveillance, cloud computing data centers, manufacturing facilities, R&D research labs, and training. There are trade relationships with at least 47 of the 54 countries in Africa. Its digital footprint is, to a great extent, a function of the fact that 41 of the continent's countries are signatories to China's Belt and Road Initiative. The Digital Silk Road segment of the BRI focuses on internet connectivity, artificial intelligence, the digital economy, telecommunications, smart cities, and cloud computing. As an example of the incursion of the Chinese initiative into Africa, its investments in the Digital Silk Road programs in the five nations of Angola, Ethiopia, Nigeria, Zambia, and Zimbabwe alone total $8.43 billion.

Researchers have estimated that as a result of BRI agreements "over 6,000 of China's internet enterprises [in addition to] . . . over 10,000 Chinese technological products have gained access to overseas markets." Many of these assets are being used to enhance connectivity and create a digital infrastructure to allow the countries to modernize their economies.

The success of the incursion of Chinese high technology firms into Africa can be attributed to two principal factors. The first is that their goods are relatively inexpensive when compared to those manufactured in the West. The second is that Chinese manufacturers market their products in the African markets in ways in which neither the American nor Western European manufacturers do. In fact, the Chinese are capable of meeting the short deadlines on goods and services sometimes imposed upon them with which the West cannot compete and at prices that are not only beyond competitive but sometimes represent a short-term loss as an investment against a long-term gain. The Chinese were simply cultivating not only a market but a demand for their goods and services at rates of speed and at prices with which the West could not or would not compete.

But there was a payoff that would never be reflected on a firm's, or nation's, balance sheet. As the West had learned the hard way, Chinese software and hardware both integrated "back doors" which allowed them full access to any and all data collected. Signals Intelligence, or SIGINT, in the form of either words or images, could often prove invaluable. And Africa was nothing more than their proving ground. As Zhang Yanmeng, ZTE's CEO, had said when referring to Ethiopia's infrastructure, "This is the world's only project in which a national telecom network is built by a sole equipment supplier." Similarly, Australian researchers had written about "data colonialism in Zimbabwe" and spoken about how an agreement between China's Cloudwalk Technology and the Zimbabwean government had facilitated sending biometric data on "millions of its citizens to China to assist in the development of facial recognition algorithms that work with different ethnicities and will therefore expand the export market for China's product." Huawei's description of their Kenyan Safe City project enumerated 1,800 HD cameras and 200 HD traffic surveillance systems distributed across the country's capital city, Nairobi. The national police command center supported over 9,000 police officers and 195 police stations. With Huawei's HD video surveillance and a visualized integrated command solution, the efficiency of policing efforts as well as detention rates rose significantly. In Uganda, security officials purchased a Huawei facial recognition system costing $126 million.

Africa had proven an ideal location to appeal to government officials, be they dictators or benign monarchs. But China had bigger fish to fry. The technological success of Chinese products had earned them respect around the world. They could now dispatch their governmental emissaries in the form of representatives of the Ministry of Foreign Affairs to market their Digital Silk Road technology throughout Western Europe.

Chapter Three

Western Europe is one of the most technologically-advanced regions on the face of the Earth. Making exceptions for a handful of metropolitan areas such as Hong Kong, it would be second only to the United States. If one considered the strategic capabilities of smartphones, personal computers, and the internet, it was susceptible to an aggressive and malicious social media campaign by any foreign adversary.

In 1906 President Teddy Roosevelt was asked by an aide, Lieutenant Douglas MacArthur, "to what he attributed his popularity." Roosevelt replied, "To put into words what is in their hearts and minds but not in their mouths." Sixty-three years later, when referring to the Vietnam War, the phrase reappeared. An aide to President Richard Nixon had a plaque on his wall on which was engraved, "When you've got them by the balls, their hearts and minds will follow." Whether this was meant to refer to the Vietnamese or the American public we will never know.

In 2021, the saying could be paraphrased as "When you've got them by social media, their hearts and minds will follow." And the Chinese knew it. Between 2007 and 2019, household internet access in the countries of the European Union rose from 55% to 90%. Moreover, smartphone penetration in the EU was booming. Of the five nations in the world with the highest smartphone usage, four of them, the United Kingdom (82.9%), Germany (79.9%), France (77.5%), and Spain (74.3%) were in Western Europe. The third in the rankings was the United States (79.1%).

And, finally, there was social media exposure. As of 2019, the Western European figure was at 65% and rising rapidly. The three most popular sites were Facebook, Twitter, and Instagram. Facebook is an online social media and social networking service based in Menlo Park, California. It numbers 2.8 billion subscribers as of the end of 2020. That is over 36% of the world's population.

The second most popular social media service in Western Europe was Twitter. It is a microblogging and social networking service on which users post and interact with messages known as "tweets". It is based in San Francisco, California. Registered users can post, like, and retweet tweets, but unregistered users can only read them. Users access Twitter through its website interface or its mobile-device application software, or "app". Twitter has 330 million subscribers, roughly equivalent to the population of the United States, accommodates 340 million tweets a day, and handles an average of 1.6 billion search queries daily.

Instagram is a photograph- and video-sharing social networking service, not surprisingly owned by Facebook. It lets users upload media that can be edited with filters and sorted using hashtags and geographical tagging. Posts can be shared publicly or with pre-approved followers. Users can browse other users' content by tags and locations and view trending content. In 2018 it had 1 billion registered users, nearly one out of every seven people in the world.

As an insight into the perception of political entities as to the persuasive power of social media, in March of 2021 the government of India threatened to jail employees of both Facebook and Twitter in an attempt to decrease or negate political protests and exercise far-ranging powers over free speech. The threat was in response to the two tech companies' failure to comply with the government's requests to delete posts and data which supported opposition movements and their attempts to influence or attack prevailing public policies. The population of India is 1.352 billion while that of the European Union only approaches 448 million, but the social media penetration in the EU was such that the posts and data appearing there had an inordinate impact upon the public's perception of EU policies' effects upon their daily lives.

There was a movement afoot in the European Union to ban the sale of Huawei and ZTE telecommunication equipment, both manufactured in the People's Republic of China. The expressed justification was that European-manufactured equipment was all that was needed and that it would create jobs for Europeans and revenue for European companies and their home nations in taxes. But Europe was well into the transition from 4G (fourth generation) to 5G networks and smartphones. And, already, the two Chinese vendors had a combined market share in the European Union of more than 40%.

Calculations had been done showing that a ban on Chinese telecom equipment would add $62 billion in costs to the creation of the EU's 5G networks and delay their completion by as much as 18 months. But astute techies and politicians knew full well that the insinuation of Chinese manufacturers' products into the pipeline for smartphones, network hardware, and the enabling software could have a far more crucial impact upon the EU than simply economic.

The report which yielded the $62 billion figure went much further. "Half of this (additional cost) would be due to European operators being impacted by higher input costs following significant loss of competition in the mobile equipment market. Additionally, operators would need to replace existing infrastructure before implementing 5G upgrades. We offer a technical solution whereby we can overlay our 5G equipment on top of another vendor's 4G gear. This solution could reduce the cost and complexity of vendor changes."

But what the report had failed to account for, or even address, was the strategic intelligence value of a 5G telecom network and internet composed of components manufactured in China. Huawei is a Chinese multinational corporation headquartered in Shenzen. It designs, develops, and markets telecommunications equipment and consumer electronics, principally smartphones. It conducts business in over 170 countries.

In 2012, Huawei became the world's largest telecommunications equipment manufacturer and in 2018 surpassed Apple as the second largest smartphone manufacturer behind Samsung. In 2020 it overtook Samsung. However, concerns exist due to the perception of state support, potential links with the People's Liberation Army, and cybersecurity concerns.

ZTE is a Chinese technology company, which is also located in Shenzen, that is partially state-owned that specializes in telecommunications and was founded in 1985. It operates carrier networks and terminals. Its core businesses are wireless, exchange, optical transmission, data telecommunications gear, telecommunications software, and smartphones.

ZTE created a new business model as a "state-owned and private-operating" economic entity. Ties to the state notwithstanding, the firm evolved into the publicly traded ZTE Corporation. By 2008, ZTE had achieved a global customer base with sales in 140 countries. ZTE has filed 48,000 patents globally, with more than 13,000 granted. In two consecutive years, ZTE was granted the largest number of patent applications globally, which is a first for a Chinese company.

The mixed-ownership model of ZTE was described as "a firm [which] is [a state-owned enterprise] from the standpoint of ownership, but a POE (privately owned enterprise) from the standpoint of management" by an article in *The Georgetown Law Journal*. ZTE described itself as "state-owned and private-run". Both *The South China Morning Post* and the *Financial Times* have described ZTE as state-owned. Other scholars have noted the links between ZTE's state-owned shareholders and the People's Liberation Army. As of 2012, ZTE was the world's 4th largest mobile phone vendor.

Investigations by American firms had determined that both Huawei and ZTE equipment had the potential to serve as covert intelligence devices. In technology's early days, firms in California's Silicon Valley had possessed the capacity to produce all the microprocessors and motherboards demanded by the industry. However, in the 2000s the demand exceeded their capacity and they turned to other manufacturers to produce those two components.

The Silicon Valley firms, under increased demand, turned the production of both microprocessors and motherboards over to manufacturers with the needed increased capacity. It turned out those manufacturers were located in China. This provided them the needed opportunity to capitalize on their technological superiority.

Chapter Four

The use of Chinese-made components in the infrastructure of Western Europe's internet network remained controversial throughout 2021. The intelligence agencies within most of the EU's nations were well-versed in the vast capabilities and long arm of China's intelligence apparatus. One of the more potent elements within the Communist Party of China (CPC) was the People's Liberation Army (PLA). And within the PLA lay Unit 61398 whose Military Unit Cover Designator had been assessed to be their advanced persistent threat (APT) unit.

It had been determined that Unit 61398 was the source of China's state-sponsored, computer-based propaganda outreach and hacking attacks. It was based in a 12-story office building in Shanghai. It had been referred to as APT1. It functioned under the 2nd Bureau of the PLA General Staff Department's Third Department. APT1 consisted of more than 20 APT groups. The mission of the Third and Fourth Departments was the infiltrating and manipulating foreign computer networks.

Since the majority of the suspected Chinese activities such as malware being embedded in a compromised system and the malware's controllers had taken place during business hours in the Chinese time zone, it had been surmised that the incursions had been conducted by state-sponsored hackers. As recently as 2013, the Chinese government had denied it conducted state-sponsored hacking. Indeed, Hong Lei, a spokesman for the Foreign Ministry, had said that such accusations were "unprofessional". However, it had since reversed its position and openly admitted the existence of cyberwarfare units, both civilian and military. In fact, the Chinese government was now openly boasting of its abilities in the realms of cybersurveillance and cyberwarfare.

Western nations had long ago begun to inadvertently purchase non-domestically manufactured computer components. Bids were let and purchase orders issued for computer components from domestic companies. But the demand outstripped the manufacturing capacity of the local firms so they had subcontracted the fabrication of the microchips, microprocessors, and motherboards to Chinese companies with excess production capacity.

Although suspicion concerning Chinese components had always been held, it took until the Fall of 2018 for those suspicions to be validated. On Thursday, October 4th, *Bloomberg Businessweek* ran a bombshell article on the exact manner in which Unit 61398 of the PLA had managed to ensure their ability to hack into virtually any component manufactured in China when it was installed in a foreign network. In 2015, American-based Amazon.com had begun to entertain the notion of acquiring Portland-based Elemental Technologies which wrote robust software code as it was ramping up Amazon Web Services (AWS). Elemental's programming had already been used in the software employed by the Central Intelligence Agency (CIA) to transmit drone imagery in real-time to its headquarters in Langley, Virginia.

In late Spring of 2015, as part of their due diligence before acquiring Elemental, AWS had shipped off several of Elemental's premier hardware products, custom-designed high-level servers, to a security consulting firm in Ontario, Canada for evaluation. The servers had been assembled for Elemental by Super Micro Computer, Inc., or SuperMicro, a San Jose-based company which was one of the world's largest suppliers of motherboards, the fiberglass-mounted components in computers onto which microchips were mounted and which were essentially integral components of any network node or junction. The consultants found immediate reason for considerable concern.

There, mounted on the motherboards, was a tiny microchip, arguably the size of a grain of rice, which had not been part of Elemental's original design. Not only had Elemental's servers already transmitted real-time drone imagery to the CIA, but they could be found in the American Department of Defense's data centers and in the onboard networks of the American Navy's warships. And Elemental was but one of hundreds of SuperMicro's customers.

Unit 61398 had planned and implemented an initiative

whereby a hardware backdoor the Chinese subcontractors of SuperMicro had inserted onto the chips would create a stealth doorway into any computer network. Unlike Stuxnet, malicious software which could be surreptitiously inserted into a computer at the point of manufacture or in transit, malicious hardware was far more devastating in that it could not usually be easily detected, deleted, reprogrammed, or circumvented. If undiscovered, it could eventually provide long-term stealth access to any node in Western Europe's internet network. One security consultant, Joe Grand of Grand Idea Studio, Inc., had told *Bloomberg Businessweek* that "[h]aving a well-done, nation-state-level hardware implant surface would be like witnessing a unicorn jumping over a rainbow. Hardware is just so far off the radar, it's almost treated like black magic."

Intelligence agencies throughout the European Union had been counseling their heads of state to forego the use of Chinese-made components in their new, 5G-capable communication and internet networks. But the $62 billion price tag to be incurred in doing so was a daunting obstacle. In the end, the incentive to doing business with Huawei, ZTE, and their subsidiaries proved to be insurmountable. After numerous discussions at the EU's quarterly meetings, the decision had been made to use Chinese components but to vigorously guard against their potentially malicious impact upon telecommunications in Western Europe.

All of this was done in the shadow of a cautionary and

well-publicized report by the United States' Federal Communications Commission (FCC). On Friday, March 12th, its Public Safety Homeland Security Bureau had issued a finding that listed five Chinese manufacturers of telecommunication network equipment that posed a threat to national security, consistent with requirements in the Secure and Trusted Communications Networks Act of 2019. The list was composed of Huawei Technologies Co., ZTE Corp., Hytera Communications Corp., Hangzhou Hikvision Digital Technology Co., and Dahua Technology Co.

The five Chinese companies were deemed to produce equipment and provide services that posed an unacceptable risk to national security or the security and safety of U.S. citizens. Acting FCC Chairwoman Jessica Rosenworcel had said, "This list is a big step toward restoring trust in our communications networks. Americans are relying on our networks more than ever to work, go to school, or access healthcare and we need to trust that these communications are safe and secure. This list provides meaningful guidance that will ensure that as next-generation networks are built across the country, they do not repeat the mistakes of the past or use equipment or services that will pose a threat to U.S. national security or the security and safety of Americans."

The American Secure Networks Act was enacted to compel the FCC to compile and publish a list of companies whose equipment and services posed "an unacceptable risk to national security or the security and safety of U.S. persons." The Public Safety Homeland Security Bureau was required to continuously update that list if additional communications equipment and services on the U.S. market were determined to meet the law's criteria.

Notwithstanding the FCC's findings and the vehement protestations of the European intelligence agencies, the European Union would sign an agreement with China which would give Unit 61398 the same sort of stealth hardware access to Europe's telecommunications signals, the most fundamental form of SIGINT, as that which it had possessed over previous generations of American telecommunications, both civilian and military, unclassified and classified, by virtue of the SuperMicro motherboards. SuperMicro's hardware had come from mainland China subcontractors in the same category such as Shenzen Chip OpTech Company, Ltd., Shenzen Unilumin Technology Company, Ltd., and Shenzen June Lead Technologies Company, Ltd.

As had taken place in Africa over previous years, two of the principal hardware suppliers to Europe would be Huawei and ZTE. But, unlike the SuperMicro case in the United States, Huawei and ZTE would not have to depend upon subcontractors to manufacture their hardware's motherboards. Both firms possessed the capacity to manufacture their own. And they could custom design them to collect, *or insert*, any form of communication or data that Unit 61398 or the Communist Party of China desired.

Chapter Five

The frequency spectrum auctions of 5G mobile telecom networks anticipated to take place in the 17 European Union member states in 2019 or 2020 had instigated an earlier and highly politicized debate in the EU about whether the use of Chinese 5G equipment in the critical infrastructure posed a threat to security. Although Australia, Japan, and New Zealand had followed the United States in imposing a selective ban on some Chinese telecom vendors, the member states chose to assign EU-coordinated domestic risk-reduction provisions over a ban. However, the global dispersion of Chinese 5G vendors' equipment, along with their attendant security risks, had still been able to capture a 29% share of the market.

Huawei ranked first among the top seven global telecom equipment vendors, ahead of American Cisco and Ciena, Swedish Ericsson, Finnish Nokia, South Korean Samsung, and Chinese state-owned ZTE Corporation. Huawei and ZTE, the leading Chinese companies, had benefited both from being shielded from foreign competition by means of domestic market access barriers and from national innovation policies which had first been enacted in 2006. The latter had boosted the two companies' competitive edge at home as well as their global footprint.

The two of them had set the standard for the industry,

but they had not penetrated the U.S. markets as deeply as they might have due to the hostile market climate toward them created by Congress's 2012 investigations into the risk they posed to national security. Major American telecom companies had relied upon Ericsson, Nokia, and Samsung.

By contrast, Huawei had enjoyed a significant market penetration in the EU as a result of its competitive prices and supposedly better quality. The governments had seemingly shown little awareness of the complicity between the public and private firms and the CPC. The most recently adopted U.S. legislation prohibited executive agencies from using Huawei or ZTE products and from contracting with entities using such products on national security grounds. Additionally, the United States had pressured its allies to follow suit and threatened that using Chinese equipment would lead to reduced intelligence-sharing within NATO.

Australia, a member of the "Five Eyes" intelligence alliance that included Canada, New Zealand, the United Kingdom (UK), and the U.S., had banned foreign vendors from taking part in the rollout of 5G mobile networks across the nation on security grounds. The Australian government had argued that "the involvement of vendors who are likely to be subject to extrajudicial directions from a foreign government that conflict with Australian law, may risk failure by the carrier to adequately protect a 5G network from unauthorized access or interference." New Zealand had banned Huawei from providing 5G network equipment, referring to a "significant network security risk". The enabling legislation was targeted at the European Union's governing body, the European Parliament, as source material to guide them in their decision-making process.

However, such a ban was found to be undesirable from the point of view of the EU's commitment to maintaining an open and competitive business environment with respect to the diversity of supply. Nonetheless, concern over security risks did arise from a combination of technical, political, and legal issues. As regarded the technical concerns, two opposing views had been prevalent: one was that risk-mitigating solutions for potential backdoors for the Chinese government to conduct cyberespionage and cyberattacks would be adequate remedies; the other was to dismiss these kinds of remedies based upon the argument that 5G networks operate in a very different way than 4G networks and created vulnerabilities of a different nature, blurring the lines between edge and core networks. High-risk vendors would no longer be confined to the edge, but could ultimately have an impact on the core network.

Another critical factor was the need for trust in both Huawei and ZTE as well as China's one-party regime. In this regard, the unique nature of the Chinese authoritarian political system, which lacks the rule of law and democratic oversight, was of considerable importance. China used advanced technologies for the systematic digital surveillance of its population while the EU pursued a human-centric approach to advanced technologies, with the protection of the digital rights of the individual being key. From a legal perspective, Chinese companies and individuals were obliged under penal sanctions to cooperate in intelligence gathering under the Chinese National Intelligence Law as well as under other related Chinese laws. Hence, the U.S. had claimed that China could use Huawei's 5G network gear as a Trojan horse by compelling operators to spy, steal corporate, government, or military secrets, and transmit data to the Chinese authorities. However, the U.S. had provided no evidence to substantiate this claim.

A 2018 security review by the UK's Huawei Cyber Security Evaluation Centre Oversight Board detected underlying defects in Huawei's software engineering and security processes but did not call for a ban. The UK's National Cyber Security Centre had previously found that the national security risks arising from the use of ZTE could not be mitigated. The arrest in Poland of a Huawei employee on spying charges in January 2019 had strongly undermined Huawei's trustworthiness and acted as a wake-up call for the EU. In a move geared to creating a unified and coordinated EU approach to 5G network security, EU member states had appeared to be seeking to avoid bans of telecom vendors from specific countries on national security grounds but continued to believe that the security risks were manageable. For Germany, where Huawei was a provider of core parts to telecom operators, a ban was not an option. The favored approach consisted of mitigating security risks by setting additional security requirements, e.g. the use of critical key components being made subject to certification.

Proposals for new legal provisions in France that would require full government access to suppliers' technology, such as encryption keys and code, were under discussion in the French Parliament. Italy had amended its legislation to allow the government to block contracts with non-EU telecom providers. Since EU member states had retained sole competence for matters of national security and the EU's role was merely complementary, on March 26th, 2019 the European Commission issued a non-binding recommendation on the cybersecurity of 5G networks. This followed calls by the European Parliament for a common approach to cybersecurity in its resolution of March 12th, 2019 and a similar call made in Action 9 of the EU – China strategic outlook paper of March 12th, 2019. The commission's recommendation had set out a roadmap until the end of 2019 for a coordinated Union risk assessment, based on member states' risk assessments using technical factors, and for a common set of risk-mitigating measures.

In the absence of harmonized Union law, member states had the option to declare the European cybersecurity certification scheme, due to be developed under the EU Cybersecurity Act, mandatory. The response from EU telecom vendors and various telecom lobby groups to a harmonized approach had so far been cautiously positive.

At its fifth High-Level Economic and Trade Dialogue on 5G technology on September 28th, 2015, the European Union and China had signed a landmark agreement in the worldwide race to develop 5G networks. At that time there was speculation that, by 2020, there would be more than 30 times as much mobile internet traffic as there was in 2010. The joint declaration had been signed by Günther Oettinger, European Commissioner in charge of the Digital Economy and Society, and Miao Wei, Chinese Minister of Industry and Information Technology. Oettinger had been quoted as saying, "5G will be the backbone of our digital economies and societies worldwide. This is why we strongly support and seek a global consensus and cooperation on 5G. With today's signature with China, the EU has now teamed up with the most important Asian partners in a global race to make 5G a reality by 2020. It's a crucial step in making 5G a success."

Both parties had committed to reciprocity and openness in terms of access to 5G network research funding and market access as well as in membership of Chinese and EU 5G associations. The declaration had been patterned upon comparable agreements between the European Union and both South Korea and Japan which the EU had signed in previous months. In May of that year the EU, through its Digital Single Market Strategy, had announced that the Commission was committed to improving spectrum coordination in the EU, particularly in light of the essential significance of future 5G technology.

Chapter Six

When China entered the telecommunications market in Africa, they went in with an aggressive agenda that included discounts, subsidies, and money. They entered into agreements with good and evil regimes alike. Their politics was of no concern.

Both categories of governments were anxious to modernize their telephone and internet capabilities. China was more than anxious to help bring these evolutions about and, in the process, the recipient governments discovered the numerous uses of the new technologies in the field of law enforcement. One of the principal uses of this new equipment was in the realm of surveillance.

In the benign regimes, that capacity could be used to monitor traffic congestion on city streets as well as locate and track criminals. In the oppressive regimes, the same technologies could be used for the surveillance of dissidents and suppression of subversive activities. In either case, much of the hardware and many of the operating systems employed pattern recognition software and its more subtle and advanced byproduct, facial recognition software. And the racial mix of Black, Arab, and White residents allowed the Chinese companies to better develop software that possessed the ability to handle the difficult task of distinguishing subtle facial differences within races. This feature alone would be of infinite value when employed against the somewhat homogenized citizens who populated Western Europe.

The Silk Road and, centuries later, the One Belt, One Road initiative were means by which to link China with Western Europe. The economic and cultural benefits would accrue to both. But neither mechanism would be able to totally eradicate the vulnerability of the Silk Road nor the tenuous nature of diplomatic relations with the European Union.

During the third week of March 2021, the potential vulnerability of the One Road sea route was made evident when the *Ever Given*, one of the largest container ships in the world, became grounded in the Suez Canal between the Red Sea and the Mediterranean Sea. The vessel is one of the latest classes of container carriers called the ultra-large container ships, or ULCS. It is not well known, but cargo ships travel through the Suez Canal in convoys.

The 220,000-ton, 1,312-foot long *Ever Given* was the fifth ship in a twenty-ship Northbound convoy. Waiting in the Mediterranean was a similar-sized convoy waiting to navigate the canal in the Southbound direction. As the days passed, additional convoys of ships backed up in both the Mediterranean and Red Seas. It was six days before the *Ever Given* was ultimately refloated.

Ironically, while the *Ever Given* was owned by the Taiwan-based Evergreen Marine Corporation, it had been leased to a Chinese company to carry goods from China to Rotterdam in the Netherlands, Europe's largest seaport. Thus, the largest financial loss to China was a result of its own operators. In addition, lawsuits have been filed in maritime courts against both the Taiwanese owner and the Chinese operator by the other vessels' owners and operators inconvenienced by the attendant delays.

The cause of the grounding has been attributed to a stronger-than-normal sandstorm and high crosswinds which made the containers topside act like a vast sail in turning the ship off course. "If you delay this vessel at Suez anchorage, it means you are making the ship owner to lose $60,000 per day or $3-4000 per hour of delay," said Jamil Sayegh, the Beirut agent for the shipping journal Lloyd's of London. Peter Sand, the chief shipping analyst with Bimco, the largest international shipping association representing shipowners, has said, "For decades shipping has been the invisible conveyor belt at sea, enabling large manufacturing industries like automotive to do 'just-in-time' shipments, even though from time to time shippers are calling foul in terms of the reliability of the schedule. Some production lines may be halted due to containers being caught in traffic like this."

Changing gears from the "One Road" seafaring route which is fraught with vulnerabilities and uncertainties,

39

diplomatic relations between China and the nations of the European Union pose an equally precarious risk. One day after the wayward cargo ship ran aground in the Suez Canal, several states of the European Union summoned their ambassadors from China into meetings to express their anger with the sanctions which Beijing had imposed upon their nationals and industries for allegedly spreading disinformation about, and slanderous claims against, China. Among the nations who called in their Chinese ambassadors were France, Germany, Belgium, and Denmark.

Belgian legislator Samuel Cogolati and French Member of the European Parliament Raphael Glucksmann were two of the ten 10 individuals singled out by China for punishment after the West imposed sanctions on Beijing over allegations of human rights violations in the Western state of Xinjiang. France had called in China's Ambassador Lu Shaye. During the meeting with the French Foreign Ministry's Asia Director, Bertrand Lortholary, Lu was told of Paris' displeasure with Beijing's decision to impose retaliatory sanctions on European nationals. During the previous week, the Chinese Embassy in France had warned against French legislators meeting with officials in Taiwan during an upcoming visit to China's "rogue province".

The warning had earned China a swift dressing down by France and provoked an antagonistic exchange on Twitter between the Chinese and Antoine Bondaz, a China expert at the Paris-based Foundation for Strategic Research. The

following weekend the Chinese embassy characterized Bondaz as a "small-time thug" and "mad hyena".
"It continues to be unacceptable and has crossed limits for a foreign embassy," Lortholary said, adding that Ambassador Lu's behavior had created an obstacle to improving diplomatic relations between China and France.

Germany called in Chinese Ambassador Wu Ken "for urgent talks with State Secretary Miguel Berger," according to the German Foreign Ministry. Berger "made clear the German government's view that China's sanctions against European MPs, scientists, and political institutions, as well as non-governmental organizations (NGOs), represent an inappropriate escalation that unnecessarily strains ties between the EU and China." Denmark, as well, had summoned China's ambassador. The Chinese envoy met officials at the Danish Foreign Ministry and was informed of Denmark's displeasure with the sanctions, the ministry said.

The diplomatic confrontation with China had erupted on Monday when the EU, Britain, and Canada blacklisted four former and current officials in China's Xinjiang region. The U.S. had also extended formerly imposed sanctions on those same Chinese officials. As a response, China had summoned the EU and British ambassadors to register formal objections. According to Chinese Foreign Ministry spokesperson Hua Chunying, Beijing had also protested to the United States and Canada. Hua said the sanctions were based on nothing but lies and false information disguised as legitimate representations of human rights violations.

"Such politicians are unwilling to see China's success and development, so they interfere in China's internal affairs under the pretext of human rights and use various excuses to contain China's development," Hua said. Beijing had rejected the Western allegations of human rights violations against the ethnic Muslim minority group, the Uighurs, in far-western Xinjiang, and said the United States and its allies had made make the false accusations for political purposes.

In a related development, the United Nations Human Rights Council (HRC) called on the West "to stop adopting, maintaining, or implementing unilateral coercive measures, in particular those of a coercive nature with extraterritorial effects." A resolution on the issue was approved by a majority of votes on the following Tuesday. A total of 30 countries, including Russia and China, supported the document, while fifteen nations, among them EU members, Britain, and Ukraine, voted against the resolution.

It was clear that the day-to-day diplomatic relations between the Chinese and the European Union would not necessarily proceed any more smoothly than they had in the past, but the progress in the development of the EU's 5G network and the attendant cell phone service along with the vastly improved internet connectivity would evolve nonetheless. In the final analysis, Western Europe would be at the forefront of the evolution into a 5G environment.

Chapter Seven

Had the United States not created the Federal Communications Commission (FCC) in 1930, and the control of the airwaves not been entrusted to a single unified entity, the development of the nation's 5G network would have evolved in as haphazard a manner as was taking place in Western Europe in 2022. The European Union represents 27 countries. If one were to include the other Western European nations and move into the Commonwealth of Independent States (CIS), the number of autonomous entities would exceed 50. Due to the wide range of national socioeconomic statuses and maturity of governments, coordinating any initiative is all but impossible.

Some of the first countries to make the transition to 5G were the richer ones whose consumers would not be reluctant to purchase the pricier 5G smartphones. In April 2019, Sunrise in Switzerland was the first company to launch 5G. The next was Everything Everywhere, or EE, a telecommunication company in the United Kingdom. In May of 2019, they started Britain's first 5G network. By 2020, most of the towns in the UK were covered.

In June, Vodafone launched their second network, after the one in Great Britain, in Spain. In Italy, Vodafone and Telecom Italia Mobile, also known as TIM, had 5G networks in operation, again in June. By December, fifteen companies had 5G networks in operation in nine of the European Union countries.

It was by this time that it was becoming evident that the multiplicity of telecom companies that would necessarily be involved in building a 5G network in Western Europe was not tenable. Notwithstanding the Covid-19 pandemic and its associated xenophobia, especially against the Chinese, it became apparent that having two companies, Huawei and ZTE, build the 5G core and its attendant 5G networks would not only be the most efficient method but both swifter and less costly. China and its two leading telecom firms were prepared with the equipment, loans, and subsidies to facilitate the creation of Western Europe's 5G infrastructure and supply it with a variety of 5G smartphones.

By the end of 2020, the download speeds of the 5G networks in Europe had already reached between twice and three times those of the previous 4G networks. While well below the fastest services in countries like South Korea and Saudi Arabia, it was a giant step ahead of from where it had come. At that time, users in the United Kingdom were spending only 4.5% of their time connected to 5G. The highest percentage in Europe was the Netherlands at 13.2%. At the current rate of 5G network development, reaching full broadband penetration was estimated to take as long as five years, far behind the uptake of the 4G network in Europe in its opening months of 2012. Bringing in Huawei and ZTE was expected to cut that time in half, if not less.

With Europe's 5G quandary, China's Huawei and ZTE offered a solution. Huawei, which was testing its hardware on over 154 carriers in 66 countries, would be the primary contractor and ZTE would provide a backstop in the event of a shortage in either hardware or smartphones. While some of the Western European governments still harbored suspicions that Chinese-built digital infrastructures might come with spyware and create long-term dependencies, the money was right and the speed with which the entire continent could be served by a coherent 5G network was both undeniable and irresistible.

Although at least eight European nations had signed agreements with Huawei by 2020 for the provision of a 5G infrastructure and network, many still had reservations. The fragmentation which such an approach to continent-wide coverage posed meant that Europe would continue to lag behind other technologically advanced nations. The United States and Asia were already significantly more sophisticated in their approach to establishing collaborative infrastructures.

The United States was leading in 5G wireless technology. It had made 5G a national security priority, giving it the wholehearted backing of President Robert Allen's new administration. He had even referenced it in his 2021 Inaugural Address. Nonetheless, the United States lacked the digital bandwidth that both China and South Korea possessed.

The Chinese government's financial support and its native industry's momentum had facilitated the 5G infrastructure growth. The Chinese government had long ago opened up sectors of the mid- and high-band spectrum and had authorized the release of at least an additional 100 megahertz of mid-band spectrum. South Korea had been the first nation in Asia to launch commercial 5G networks and already had a fully functioning network of consumer-level 5G services.

The European Electronic Communications Code adopted in 2018 was meant to enforce rules to dictate how to improve how its countries managed the broadband spectrum. It set out how member states must make 5G pioneer bands available by the end of 2020. This had been intended to coerce them to speed up their rollout of 5G networks. The only practical way to do this was to allow companies with a proven track record, namely Huawei and ZTE, to step in.

But European concerns were that critical infrastructure built with Chinese technology might give Chinese companies access to unlimited amounts of sensitive data and industrial information which could ultimately be turned over to the Xi Administration in Beijing. A Chinese-manufactured 5G infrastructure could subject European countries to other national security threats. Any bit of digital data or pixel of digital imagery could become subject to Chinese scrutiny and, potentially, adversarial use against any nation on the continent.

In the United Kingdom, the UK's largest telecom provider, British Telecommunications, or BT, had been working with a cybersecurity center run by Huawei known as the Huawei Cyber Security Evaluation Centre (HCSEC) since 2014 under the supervision of the National Cyber Security Centre (NCSC), part of the British government. This had been a prescient move as the 2016 presidential election in the United States had brought to power an administration bent upon taking Chinese company's to task and using them as leverage against the Chinese government. The preexisting relationship between Huawei and BT was able to weather the United States – China blowup without jeopardizing the stability of the nation's telecommunications network. The same could not be said for some of the other countries.

During his two terms in the White House, Republican John Jefferson's administration had made full use of its authority and his party's majority in the Senate to make every attempt at leveling the playing field in the realm of international trade between the United States and China. And he had used his diplomatic clout in both Eastern and Western Europe to help punish the Chinese for their past transgressions. He had done his best to dry up the markets for Chinese goods and services in Europe and manipulated the financial markets to make trade with China less attractive.

His successor, Democrat Robert Allen, was a closet pacifist. He had held off as long as possible without meeting face-to-face with Chinese President Xi Jinping, but when he finally did he made the trip to Beijing and took the opportunity to rescind most of the tariffs and trade sanctions that Jefferson had imposed upon China. Just as he had done when he withdrew American troops from Afghanistan, Allen had, in a similar fashion, extracted any teeth left in the diplomatic and financial relationship between the United States and the Chinese.

Without the threat of retaliation by the Jefferson Administration should the member states of the European Union, the other Western European nations, or the countries of the CIS choose to transact business with China's telecom firms then the door would become wide open for Huawei and ZTE to waltz into Europe and fabricate the continent's 5G infrastructure. The first 5G New Radio (NR) launches in Western Europe depended upon pairing with the existing 4G long-term evolution (LTE) infrastructure in non-standalone (NSA) mode, a 5G NR radio with a 4G core, before evolving into a full standalone (SA) mode with a 5G core network. No sooner would the Chinese-built network be in place than the People's Liberation Army begin to tap into the pipeline and the PLA's Unit 61398 be capable of reaping the intelligence benefits they had anticipated all along.

Chapter Eight

In the Twenty-first Century, one of the curses to mankind has been the evolution of the smartphone as the omnipresent target of the eyesight of the modern human being. When people go to see the grandeur of the Grand Canyon, they're staring at their smartphones. When they go to a rock concert, they're aiming their smartphones. And when they go to social gatherings or reunions, they're composing the image on the screen of their smartphones.

But the smartphone has been a boon to several endeavors. One of them has been the collection of intelligence. Its facilitator has, in many cases, been social media. In the case of state leaders, the public, be they supporters or detractors, have recorded innumerable photos and mind-numbing hours of video. The same can be said for star athletes and celebrities. Healthcare experts can use these photos and film clips to construct a profile of a leader and detect potential physical and mental deterioration. Maybe even predict an imminent death. And then there is the so-called "common man". But societies are defined by these people. And intelligence profiles of societies are made that much more reflective and evocative of their subjects by their inclusion.

But what one person may deem nothing more than a photograph or film clip, an intelligence analyst may find as a missing piece of a jigsaw puzzle or a crucial element in a vast mosaic. Aerial reconnaissance has been an integral component of warfare since the mid-1800s. Before aircraft had ever been invented, Union soldiers used hot air balloons to fly above Confederate lines, record their observations in both sketches and narratives, and return them to their commanding officers behind the lines. By the 1950s, reconnaissance satellites were taking pictures of missile silos and other military assets from 200 miles above the Earth. And aircraft from the U-2 *Dragon Lady* to the SR-71 *Blackbird*, both products of the Lockheed "Skunk Works", formally known at its inception as the Lockheed Advanced Development Projects program originally located in Burbank, California but now relocated to Palmdale, can go wherever they want, whenever they want, and photograph target sites with little or no fear.

As early as the 1960s, claims were circulating that a reconnaissance aircraft could take a photograph so detailed that one could read the headline on a newspaper being held by a man in Times Square. The only requirement was a film with a high enough resolution and a good enough lens. In the aerial reconnaissance discipline, the Holy Grail has always been the concept of "infinite resolution" film. But if it exists, it has never been acknowledged. Now smartphones and the internet may be well on the way to putting "eyes in the sky" out of business.

Let us say that the People's Liberation Army Navy

(PLAN) was surveilling American nuclear-powered submarines. Distinguishing between fast attack submarines (SSNs) and ballistic missile submarines (SSBNs) is a simple task based upon size and shape. But what if you want to know the particular submarine. Again, size and shape would tell you if it was a *Virginia* class fast attack submarine or an *Ohio* class ballistic missile submarine. But different variants possess different capabilities. Perhaps the only way to know the name of a particular boat would be to read her sail number.

Now, reading a sail number from directly overhead is not possible. And side looking photography introduces distortion depending upon the altitude and weather. But there is a source available to almost anybody, and most assuredly anyone operating the internet and a 5G network.

If you were to pick up the phone and call the Public Information Office at Naval Submarine Base New London in Groton, Connecticut and ask them to send you an email each time a submarine was leaving port or returning to port, as well as the name or sail number of the submarine, you would be told that such information is classified. Of course, you could station an observer at the mouth of the Thames River where it empties into Long Island Sound, but that would be inconvenient. There is a far better source for the same information.

At sub bases like New London, Pearl Harbor, Kings

Bay, or Kitsap (formerly Bremerton), formal announcements are made, principally for the benefit of the families of the crew, shortly before departures and arrivals. In that way, spouses and their children can see their loved ones off or welcome them home. But, in such cases, there are prominent signs throughout the docking area saying "Photography Prohibited".

In places like the Sistine Chapel or elsewhere throughout The Vatican, "Photography Prohibited" signs are widely displayed. Among other reasons, one is that the photographing detracts from the solemnity of the surroundings. But another is that, over time, the bright flashes of light alter the colors and degrade the definition of the irreplaceable paintings. Nonetheless, tourists from Japan and nuns from Africa run around trying to capture images of every painting they can. The *Polizia* and *Carabinieri* are helpless to stop them.

In the case of New London, young sons and daughters of crew members from the lowliest submariner to the highest-ranking officer can hardly be expected to resist the temptation of taking a photograph of a returning father or mother. And of course, that photo, with the vessel in the background, would have to be shared with Grandma or Granddad, either on social media or as an attachment to an email.

If a hacking unit within an intelligence or military

organization, like China's Unit 61398, had access to all smartphone transmissions and internet services, they could download a copy of such an image. Then all they would have to do is refer to *Jane's Fighting Ships* with the sail number to determine the boat's name, dimensions, armaments, silhouettes, and photographs. Why go through the time, expense, *and risk*, of sending an undercover agent to New London to take a photograph when an unsuspecting child would send one to you? As pointed out earlier, 36% of the world's population are registered users on Facebook and one out of every seven people in the world use Instagram.

There are submarine bases dispersed throughout the world. And allies share bases with one another. Tracking the whereabouts of a nation's submarines is only as hard as collecting photographs of the comings and goings of boats from allied submarine bases. The bases include those in Bahrain, Greece, Italy, Japan, South Korea, Singapore, Spain, and the United Kingdom.

The same technology could be used to evaluate the type and strength of an adversary's ground forces and air forces. Armies routinely hold "Open Houses" to proudly display their latest hardware to an adoring public. And air forces do the same. Even "closed" bases give up their security and secrecy from time to time to allow the public in. Only they suspend operations so as not to reveal too much of their mission or classified capabilities.

But, once again, innocent members of the public would become unwitting assets for the enemy by snapping photos of every tank and aircraft and posting them on social media or sending them to friends and family as attachments to an email. There was no longer a need to surveil enemy installations to get images of the latest in arms. They could simply continue to monitor the telecommunications networks and wait for the images to come to them.

As long ago as at least the 1960s, the military-industrial complex had collaborated with the U.S. Army to form a grant-funded program which had, by now, come to be known as the Submillimeter Wave Technology Laboratory. It was housed in the abandoned, red-brick Wannalancit woolen mill beside one of the canals which ran through Lowell, Massachusetts, and emptied into the Merrimack River. It operated under the auspices of the University of Massachusetts – Lowell and was funded, on paper, by the National Ground Intelligence Center, a unit of the U.S. Army Intelligence and Security Command, located in Charlottesville, Virginia.

The lab employed a staff who built hyper-accurate scale models of both domestic and foreign military equipment from artillery to tanks and everything in between. Every external angle of the surface was exact and the density of the materials mimicked those of the actual weapon. Once those models were completed, they were placed on a pedestal in an insulated room with radar-absorbing materials lining the walls and ceiling. Then radar waves with submillimeter accuracy were used to create a 360° computer image file.

Once a file was completed, it was added to the military's radar targeting "package". That package was then downloaded to units like the 480th Intelligence, Surveillance, and Reconnaissance Wing at Langley Air Force Base to be used by Imagery Analysts to identify foreign military equipment. But it was also uploaded to the targeting radar units in Army ground weapons like tanks and Air Force combat aircraft. In that way, they could instantaneously determine if a ground vehicle belonged to friend or foe. It immediately yielded a display providing the weapons officer with the target's offensive and defensive capabilities. And it helped in preventing "friendly fire" incidents.

Those targeting packages were distributed over ostensibly "secure" network lines, but hackers could intercept them and know everything needed about an enemy's weaponry as well as what the enemy believed it knew about the intercepting country's arms. By reverse-engineering the data in a targeting package, the enemy could create a three-dimensional image of a weapon using selected points on the "skeleton" of the radar image. That "x-ray" of the weapon could then be translated into a black & white image and that image inserted into its pattern recognition software. In that way, images from an Open House would become the enabling trigger to identify any piece of military hardware whose capabilities would be well-cataloged in Jane's publications or Wikipedia.

One thing a single image captured on the internet or in an email could not do is count the number of any submarine, tank, or aircraft at a particular installation. Submarine bases have piers, army bases have armories, and air force bases have hangars. But using reconnaissance satellite imagery, or even Google Earth images, one could count the number of storage facilities and record their dimensions. Knowing the weapon's dimensions, one could calculate how many tanks an armory could hold or how many of an aircraft could fit in a hangar. By doing so, the enemy could determine the *maximum* number of a piece of hardware could be present at a facility.

In the case of warships and submarines, things get a little weirder. You can't hide an aircraft carrier. And most vessels, not even the smallest, cannot fit inside a larger ship. But then there are the submarines. Many sub bases put canopies over the flooded areas between piers. The canopies may be camouflaged or not to match the color and texture of the water beneath. The purpose of this is obvious. A submarine may be in that pier or maybe not. Aerial reconnaissance would be unable to determine the presence of another object beneath an opaque one. But the enemy would be forced to consider the possibility that the slip was occupied. There are tricks to evading surveillance, but they only conceal the size of the enemy, not its presence.

Chapter Nine

Whether in business, diplomacy, or warfare, the Chinese have always been known for playing the long game. They think not in terms of years nor even decades, but rather in terms of centuries. Political scientists and military strategists know this well from experience. It had taken China seven decades to move on Taiwan, a battle which would have seemed to require only years to win.

Thus it was to be with the psychological war fought with digital weapons in Europe. Sun Tzu, a Taoist philosopher, military strategist, and general is best known for his book *The Art of War* which he wrote in the sixth century B.C. Its most famous quote: "Every battle is won or lost before it's ever fought."

As early as the mid-1980s, it was becoming evident that the internet would have an enormous impact on people's behaviors. And ever since 2012, President Xi Jinping had been meeting regularly with Ren Zhengfei, the founder and Chief Executive Officer of Huawei, and Hou Weigu, the leader of ZTE, to discuss and speculate upon the potential uses of the internet to influence societal development, both at home and abroad. Even after 2016 when 75-year-old Hou retired from his formal role as Chairman of the firm, he continued to be one of the three principals in these meetings.

These three men saw the internet as a way to put China's imprint upon nations near and far. Because Africa was the least technologically advanced continent, they chose it as a proving ground for Huawei and ZTE's latest 5G products and services. And whether employed for good or evil, there was little doubt that these two company's output changed its way of life.

But Africa was not China's target of choice. Having had its products banned or their uses restricted in the United States, the member states of the European Union posed the most influential and lucrative cohesive destination for China's digital culture. And with that income and cultural influence, China could forever alter the course of development in Western Europe throughout the Twenty-first Century and beyond.

At the first meeting of the three Chinese oligarchs in Beijing, the subject of the European Union was brought up by the group's senior member, Hou Weigu of ZTE, who was the first to speak after drinks were poured all around and the meeting was called to order.

"This European Union," began Hou, "It puts me in mind of the Soviet Union. A community of culturally disparate states held together by economic interests and fear. In the case of the Soviet Union, it was held together by the relative economic strength of Russia and the fear of its strength. As I see it, the European Union is, in the first instance, held together by the collective economic strength of the group but, in reality, propped up by a handful, among them Germany, France, and Great Britain.

"The concepts that stand out to me are 'community' and 'collective', again reminiscent of the Soviet Union. I don't find it coincidental that the Soviet Union fell in 1991 and the Maastricht Treaty, which created the European Union, was signed in 1992. I find the parallels striking and the vulnerabilities moreso."

"Is there a point you're trying to make, Weigu?" asked Ren Zhengfei of Huawei.

"Indeed there is," said Hou. "Because of their inherent weaknesses, the majority of the member states need the community, the collective strength of the whole, to survive. And 'community' is the root word of 'Communism'. What I see is a group of nations in need of Communism. A community needs an infrastructure, and in the Twenty-first Century that infrastructure derives from the internet and the telecommunications network."

"And between the two of you," interjected President Xi, "you can offer the EU the infrastructure they need. Brilliant! So how do we corner the market on their telecommunications industry?"

"How, indeed?" responded Hou. "That is where you

come in, Mister President. Subsidies, financing, and grants. Between Huawei and ZTE, Zhengfei and I can provide the infrastructure. If you and the state can make the economics attractive enough to them, they'll go for it.

"We wanted to go for the United States, but their President Jefferson raised too many objections. However, there is too much divisiveness among Berlin, Paris, and London for them to present a united front. All we would have to do is come in faster and under the cost of any other telecom companies and they'd be hard-pressed to reject our offer in the face of the citizenry's scrutiny."

"And what would be the next step?" inquired Xi.

"We would exert our influence and powers, both known and unrevealed, to both collect and disseminate information," said Hou. "The collection would be in the realms of the political stability and military power of the member states of the European Union. That task would be handled by Unit 61398 of the PLA and their findings would be distributed to a small group of influential leaders and their aides in China.

Second, as for dissemination of information, it would take two forms. One would be in the low-key promotion of Chinese-made products. This would increase their marketability within the European Union and its neighboring countries and the financial benefits would accrue to native companies and, ultimately, to China itself. The third, and perhaps most significant, role would be to subtly introduce into European daily life and discourse an appreciation of the bedrock principles upon which the People's Republic of China is built.

"The BBC had a virtual monopoly in the industry of television broadcasting in Great Britain for a number of years and, with the exception of the so-called pirate radio stations, radio broadcasting as well. It massaged the news and censored the music. The people heard and saw what the government wanted them to hear and see. In the United States, CNN did much the same thing when it came to broadcasting news and distributing it on the internet. As the operators of the internet with control over the nuances of the content being disseminated, we could slowly desensitize the residents of Europe to the underpinnings of the PRC for which they have been conditioned to have an aversion. Over time we could come to be viewed as a potential ally instead of a feared enemy. That is when we could seize the opportunity to exert as great an influence as we so chose over day-to-day life in the West."

"Do you really think all this would be so easy to accomplish, Weigu?" asked Xi, somewhat incredulously.

"In the short term, 'No'," said Hou. "But we Chinese are not in this battle for the short term. If this plan is executed slowly, over time, with great finesse, we could transform Europe's vision of China from an adversarial superpower into a benign, and possibly even palatable, partner."

"I like what I hear you saying," said Xi. Then, turning to Ren, Xi asked, "What say you, Zhengfei?"

"Weigu and I have spoken of this for many years; perhaps now for over a quarter of a century. But our nation's leadership was not right. Now, with you at the helm, we believe that China has the right man in the right place and that the time has come to exert not only our industry's but our country's power to influence future national and international events.

"The fiasco over Taiwan was an embarrassment for all Chinese. We must put it in the back of people's minds. Our military must be permitted to take its rightful place in the world with our form of government and our country along with it."

"I must give this some serious thought," said Xi. "But, in any event, I will, as you have asked, see that the extension of attractive financing options is made available to the EU nations to entice them to purchase and employ both your products and your services. I will need to consult my Central Military Commission, but I believe they will like what they hear. Until we meet again, feel free to proceed with the marketing of your products and services to the EU."

Chapter Ten

In April of 2021, prior to the anticipated widespread rollout of 5G technology, networks, and internet applications, Ursula von der Leyen, President of the European Commission, the executive branch of the European Union, released a plan to impose rules regulating permitted uses of artificial intelligence (AI) within the telecommunications infrastructure of its 27 member states. European Union representatives stated that uses of artificial intelligence that threaten people's safety or rights such as live facial recognition should be prohibited. The EU is in a race to catch up with the technological developments coming out of the United States and China.

The EU's proposals are an effort to allow its 27 member states to maintain their status as the world's standard-bearer for technology regulation. They employ a four-level "risk-based approach" in an effort to balance privacy rights and the agenda of encouraging innovation. "With these landmark rules, the EU is spearheading the development of new global norms to make sure AI can be trusted," said Margrethe Vestager, the European Commission's Executive Vice President for the Digital Age. "By setting the standards, we can pave the way to ethical technology worldwide and ensure that the EU remains competitive along the way."

Previous EU technology regulation efforts have earned it a reputation as a pioneer in the field. They have included filing antitrust challenges against Silicon Valley giants like Google. These actions were taken under the leadership of Vestager, also the EU's Competition Chief, years before such aggressive gestures had become either fashionable or commonplace. Nonetheless, Google still maintains its 36% share of the world's social media market.

Under the AI proposals, there is prohibition in principle on controversial "remote biometric identification," also known as facial recognition, in real time because "there is no room for mass surveillance in our society," Vestager said. There would, however, be narrowly defined exceptions within the field of law enforcement such as searching for a missing child or wanted person, or in the event of attempting to prevent a terrorist attack. But even those carve-outs are controversial. Patrick Breyer, an EU Pirate Party lawmaker, has said that biometric and mass surveillance technology "in our public spaces undermines our freedom and threatens our open societies. We cannot allow the discrimination of certain groups of people and the false incrimination of countless individuals by these technologies."

Herbert Swaniker, a technology lawyer, has stated that with "General Data Protection Regulation (GDPR), we saw the EU's rules reach every corner of the world and apply pressure on countries globally to reach a new international gold standard. We can expect this also for AI regulation.

This is just the beginning." The Commission envisions establishing a European Artificial Intelligence Board to enforce the regulations. Violations would bear potential fines of up to more than $36,000 or, for companies, up to 6% of their global annual revenue, whichever is higher.

EU Competition Chief Vestager went on to say that, "With these landmark rules, the EU is spearheading the development of new global norms to make sure AI can be trusted. By setting the standards, we can pave the way to ethical technology worldwide and ensure that the EU remains competitive along the way." But the proposal has met with resistance from all sides, with Big Tech claiming that the proposed regulations could stifle development while civil liberties groups complain that the proposals have too many "loopholes".

The EU's Internal Market Commissioner, Thierry Breton, has said, "Today's proposals aim to strengthen Europe's position as a global hub of excellence in AI from the lab to the market." Some features of the regulations would include making "generalized surveillance" out of bounds as well as the use of AI to "manipulate the behavior, opinions or decisions" of citizens. While real-time facial recognition would be prohibited except in extraordinary cases, the military use of artificial intelligence would be exempted.

Christian Borggreen, a tech lobbyist from the

Computer and Communications Industry Association, has said that his constituency welcomes the EU's "risk-based" approach, but cautioned against handcuffing the industry. "We hope the proposal will be further clarified and targeted to avoid unnecessary red tape for developers and users." But civil libertarians have stated that the regulations are insufficient to prevent abuses of emerging technologies. Orsolya Reich, speaking for the group Liberties, said, "Although the proposal technically bans the most problematic uses of AI, there are still loopholes for member states to go through to get around the bans. There are way too many problematic uses of the technology that are allowed, such as the use of algorithms to forecast crime or to have computers assess the emotional state of people at border control."

* * *

It was ironic that in 2021 the European Union was beginning to address technologies and applications which had been employed by the Chinese since 2010 or before, and which they were planning to use over the Chinese-built 5G network infrastructure and smartphones. It was like closing the barn door after the horse had run away. China had been creating advanced persistent threat units, or APTs, for over two decades. As of 2021, the computer and internet watchdog company FireEye had identified, in addition to APT1, also known as Unit 61398, 27 additional advanced persistent threat units.

These units had all been given code names by both the United States intelligence establishment and NATO. Those names were sometimes indicative of the work the unit had been tasked to perform and at other times simply whimsical. Nonetheless, they all existed and were all state-sponsored by China and a significant threat to Western national security.

FireEye had compiled the most authoritative and comprehensive inventory of the Chinese APTs.

APT1 was codenamed "Comment Crew" as its approach was to leave malicious software in attachments or hyperlinks included in the "Comments" section of the website of a target agency or company. Its target groups include those engaged in Information Technology, Aerospace, Satellites and Telecommunications, and Scientific Research and Consulting.

APT2 was focused on Military and Aerospace organizations. Its principal means of attack was "spear phishing". Spear phishing is an email or electronic communications scam targeted towards a specific individual, organization, or business. Although often intended to steal data for malicious purposes, cybercriminals may also intend to install malware on a targeted user's computer.

APT3, or "UPS Team", targets Aerospace and Defense entities. The phishing emails used by APT3 are usually generic in nature, almost appearing to be spam. Attacks have exploited an unpatched vulnerability in the way Adobe Flash Player parses Flash Video files. APT4, known as "Maverick Panda", focuses on Aerospace and Defense and uses spear phishing. APT6 targets Electronics and Telecommunications entities. It uses customized backdoors which have been inserted into the software of the target organization to bypass the conventional firewalls.

APT7 targets Aerospace and Defense and APT8 does the same. APT9 focuses on Aerospace and Defense as well as Pharmaceuticals and Biotechnology. APT10, or "Menupass Team", aims at Aerospace and Telecom firms as well as government agencies in the United States, Europe, and Japan. APT12, the "Calc Team", targets the Defense Industrial Base and Journalists.

The list goes on and on up to APT41. Other targets include Economic interests, Taiwanese organizations, International Law Firms, Information Technology companies, Media and Government in the Philippines, members of the Association of Southeast Asian Nations (ASEAN), and countries in the Belt and Road Initiative.

There would soon be a new advanced persistent threat unit focused upon the economic, governmental, and military cultures of the member states of the European Union. And then there would be the subtle inclusion of the PRC culture. Insinuated into the other threats, it would never be noticed.

Chapter Eleven

By May of 2022, the 5G rollout was in full swing in the European Union. Some countries were blanketed while in others the coverage was still sporadic. In those areas, legacy 4G was still the standard, however the 5G-capable smartphones were well-equipped to handle both. But, most significantly, the Huawei and ZTE core hardware and operating software were fully deployed and as much information was flowing to and from the Advanced Persistent Threats units in China as was being exchanged within the EU.

Always preeminent in the minds of China's leadership was military superiority. It wasn't that they did not have excellent military scientists and engineers. It was only that they spent their valuable time fine-tuning the work of others rather than performing the fundamental design work themselves.

It had been documented that China either stole or paid for the classified proprietary information and intellectual property of others rather than go through the drudgery of developing it themselves. Most often that information came from the United States. But today's targets would be the military-industrial leaders of the European Union.

Although the bulk of the military hacking to be

performed by Chinese APTs would take place under the auspices of the People's Liberation Army, it was the Air Force and Navy which would be the principal beneficiaries. The PLA's primary war machine was their over 4,000 Type 99 MBT main battle tanks, and revolutionary advances in tank technology were few and far between. But the introduction of new defensive technologies in warships was far more frequent while both offensive and defensive breakthroughs in fifth-generation aircraft seemed to arise overnight and build upon one another. China would hack the files of the manufacturers for the EU's navies and air forces to pick up advanced warning of their latest innovations so that they could develop workarounds before they ever became operational.

APTs 1, 2, 3, and 7 in China, among others, would be focused on the aerospace and maritime military manufacturers in the European Union. Some would specialize on the companies which had manufactured the EU's newest aircraft carrier, the *Charles de Gaulle*, while others would zero in on the companies which had produced the Swedish SAAB JAS 39 *Gripen*, French Dassault *Rafale*, and the Eurofighter *Typhoon*, a multi-role, air superiority fighter, manufactured by Airbus, BAE Systems, and Leonardo, all fourth-generation multi-role fighters. They were the most likely candidates to be coming up with the latest innovations to be incorporated into the EU's fifth-generation fighter aircraft.

The Digital Silk Road

The construction of the *Charles de Gaulle*, the flagship of the French Navy, was begun in 1987. It had not been completed until 2000. It was a nuclear-powered aircraft carrier that was a product of Direction des Construction Navales (DCNS) in the port city of Brest. DCNS is a French defense contractor which specializes in naval-based defense platforms. The group employs nearly 13,000 people in 18 countries.

Even though DCNS, or Naval Group, had numerous military contracts, many of them involving classified information, their corporate computer firewalls were no challenge for the Chinese hackers. The technology aboard the nuclear-powered *Charles de Gaulle* did not qualify as state-of-the-art. That distinction went to the carriers HMS *Queen Elizabeth II* and HMS *Prince of Wales* of the United Kingdom and the USS *Gerald R. Ford* of the United States. But the *Charles de Gaulle* was the most advanced and formidable warship in the European Union. French President Marine Le Pen had declared that a new carrier was in the works, but it was not expected to be commissioned until 2038. The Chinese hackers would be targeting not only DCNS but any contractors which were subsequently announced to be working on the next generation of French carrier.

There were only two other EU warships that would warrant Chinese attention. The first was the FREMM (short for *Frégate européenne multi-mission* or European multi-

71

purpose frigate which had been first commissioned in 2012) and the MKS 180 frigate which was not scheduled to go into service until 2028. The manufacturers of the MKS 180 would attract the majority of the attention from the Chinese APTs.

The FREMM had been designed by Fincantieri, an Italian ship designer and the largest shipbuilding company in Europe, and DCNS for the Italian and French navies respectively. Italy had ordered 10 and France 8. They were gas-turbine-propelled with electronically-scanned radar arrays, anti-air missiles, anti-ship missiles, and torpedoes for anti-submarine warfare (ASW). The frigates carried one or two helicopters which were armed with torpedoes or anti-ship missiles.

The MKS 180 frigate, on the other hand, would be built for the German Navy. This class of frigate will be mission modular, meaning that different variants or weaponry packages will be designed to perform specific tasks. They will all carry multi-function defensive radar as well as multi-function targeting radar. They will be armed with anti-air, anti-ship, and land-attack missiles. Each will carry one or two helicopters. In January 2020, the initial Requests for Proposals (RFPs) having been released five years earlier, the German Navy awarded the contract for the construction of the first round of frigates to the Dutch Damen Group. However, it was agreed that the vessels themselves would be constructed at the Blohm & Voss shipyards in Hamburg, Germany. Moreover, the information technology, radar, and fire control systems would be developed by the Thales Group, a French multinational company, at its design facilities and manufacturing plants in the Netherlands and Germany, two of the founding member states of the European Union.

The Chinese had come far in mastering the art of ship hull-building. They had constructed two of their own aircraft carriers in addition to the Russian-built carrier which they had purchased before the Russians got around to scuttling it. Much of their expertise had been derived from the construction of their massive container carriers traversing the Silk Road and Polar Silk Road routes. They had also made great strides in the building of submarines.

Nonetheless, the Chinese had hacked into the security surveillance cameras keeping watch over the maritime shipyards in the European Union. Whatever techniques which had been developed by the Europeans would be incorporated into the subsequent warships to be constructed domestically. Thus, the Chinese warships and submarines to be built in the future would be the equal of, or superior to, those of the European Union nations.

In the Spring of 2021, the People's Liberation Army Navy had sent a flotilla of Chinese container carriers with destroyer escorts through the Northern Sea Route, which they referred to as the Polar Silk Road, along the Russian

Arctic Coast to three ports on Greenland's West Coast. They had previously rebuilt the three ports to accommodate both supercarriers and naval vessels. The United States Navy, at the direction of the National Security Council, had felt compelled to eliminate the destroyers in the Western Atlantic waters and taken the rescued sailors captive until a hostage exchange agreement had been negotiated with China.

On May 6th, 2021, General Stephen Townsend, the top commander for U.S. military operations in Africa, had said Chinese officials had been approaching countries stretching from Mauritania to South of Namibia in search of where to position a naval facility on the West Coast of the African continent as a base from which to project its force closer to Western Europe *and* the United States. "They're looking for a place where they can rearm and repair warships," he said. "That becomes militarily useful in a conflict."

It was clear that China was preparing to make good on its designs on the European Union and that the U.S. could well be their next target once the domination of the European Union was accomplished. From the West Coast of Africa, Chinese military vessels could sail unobstructed along the coasts of Portugal, Spain, France, Belgium, The Netherlands, Denmark, and Norway, all of which were members of the European Union except for Norway. And, of course, Ireland would be at sea, both literally and figuratively. With their naval base in Djibouti, the Chinese could engulf the states with Mediterranean coasts as well.

Chapter Twelve

While advancements and innovations in maritime
military hardware, except for railguns and electro-magnetic
pulse (EMP) weapons, evolved at an exceedingly slow pace,
the same could not be said for military aircraft. The most
advanced fighters in the inventories of the European Union
nations, the Swedish *Gripen*, French *Rafale*, and Eurofighter
Typhoon, were all fourth-generation aircraft. The fifth-
generation fighters were in development across the
continent.

At the time, America's Lockheed Martin F-22 *Raptor*
was the acknowledged leading fifth-generation fighter
aircraft in the world. By buying off engineers at Lockheed
Martin or using leverage in the form of threats against the
families of Chinese engineers on the firm's payroll, the PLA
had obtained the plans for the *Raptor*. One only needed to
analyze the latest Chinese fighter aircraft, the Chengdu J-20
Mighty Dragon, to see that the proprietary information and
intellectual property of Lockheed Martin had been
compromised to design and manufacture the J-20.

Thus, the race was on. SAAB, Dassault, Airbus, BAE
Systems, Leonardo, and Chengdu were all in competition to
come up with the innovation or innovations which would
place their sponsor's aircraft at the head of the line in the
lineup of the latest fighter aircraft. And China was willing

to use its control of the European Union's telecom system, its access to every one of the EU's webcams, and the necessary money and familial leverage to come out ahead in the pursuit of the next lead fighter in the competition.

On May 12th, 2021, General C. Q. Brown, the Chief of Staff of the U.S. Air Force, had announced that the *Raptor* would not be America's principal fighter in the coming years. That responsibility would be distributed among the F-35 *Lightning II*, the F-15EX *Eagle II*, the F-16 *Fighting Falcon*, and the Next Generation Air Dominance, or NGAD, fighter. "Right now we have seven fighter fleets," Brown said. "My intent is to get down to about four . . ."

Brown had said the fighter makeup is "really a four-plus-one, because we're going to have the A-10 for a while as we re-wing" the *Warthog* to extend its service life into the 2030s. The role of the *Raptor* was to be taken on by the NGAD fighter. The Air Force had a complement of 186 *Raptors* with an average age of 12 years making it the youngest component in the fleet. Unfortunately, its mission capability rate had fallen well below expectations. Even the *Lightning II* had proven to be problematic as its multiple versions had caused issues with respect to interoperability.

The Air Force was reevaluating its fighter mix in light of its ever-changing mission. It was looking "across the board [at] all of [its] . . . combat aircraft, . . . [its] fighter portfolio. I'm really looking for a window of options," said

Brown, "because the facts and assumptions based on a threat will change over time. But I want to get us shaped in a direction . . ."

John "JV" Venable, a former F-16 pilot and a Senior Fellow at the Heritage Foundation's Center for National Defense, had said, "They never get the numbers they expect when they downsize to save money first. The numbers of tactical airframes are already too small and the service can't afford to suffer another cost-saving move that results in it getting even smaller. The F-35 was supposed to replace the F-16 and the A-10," he said. "How the service justifies acquiring a new combat-equipped 4th-gen platform, the F-15EX, defies logic."

While the turmoil within the Air Force was taking place in the E-Ring of the Pentagon regarding the composition of the American fighter fleet, the Chinese were more concerned with the European Union and its numerous air force units. They concentrated their focus on the manufacturers which had been awarded the contracts for the EU's next fleets of fifth-generation fighter aircraft. That gave them plenty of corporate firewalls to penetrate and webcams to monitor.

The SAAB aircraft development and manufacturing of the successor to the JAS 90 *Gripen* would take place in Linköping, Sweden. While their computers were well-secured, their firewalls could not withstand the hacking skills of the Chinese APTs. As for their in-house closed-circuit television system, their webcams could be accessed via the telecom node in Stockholm, just over a hundred miles to the Northeast.

The French *Rafale* had fulfilled its purpose. But that purpose had been superseded. In 1988, Dassault, the manufacturer of the French *Rafale,* had become Aerospatiale, a division of Airbus. The corporate headquarters for the production of military aircraft of Airbus was located in Ottobrunn, Germany. As with SAAB, the Chinese APTs hacked their way into the firm's computers while the webcams were accessed by way of the node in Munich, six miles Northwest of Ottobrunn.

Finally, the Eurofighter *Typhoon* was a twin-engine, delta wing, multirole fighter. It was originally designed as an air superiority fighter and was manufactured by a consortium of Airbus, BAE Systems, and Leonardo. The *Typhoon* entered operational service in 2003 and was in service with the air forces of Austria, Italy, Germany, and Spain.

The *Typhoon* had been a highly agile aircraft for its day, but the next generation of dogfighters had evolved and its lifespan had run its course. Moreover, a new generation of missiles had been developed which could outperform its *Brimstones* and *Storm Shadows*. The *Brimstone* was a high-explosive anti-tank (HEAT) missile used by the German Air

Force while the *Storm Shadow*, or in France SCALP EG, was a general-purpose long-range cruise missile with a Bomb Royal Ordnance Augmented Charge (BROACH).

In 1979, when Sweden decided that it needed a new generation of fighter aircraft to succeed its *Drakens* and *Viggens*, the government had begun a study calling for a versatile platform capable of "JAS", standing for *Jakt* (air-to-air), *Attack* (air-to-surface), and *Spaning* (reconnaissance), indicating a multirole fighter that could perform multiple roles during the same mission. The result was the *Gripen*. To design the successor to the *Gripen*, SAAB would form a team led by SAAB Aeronautics head Lennard Sindha. The powerplant would be developed by GKN Aerospace Engine Systems, formerly Volvo Aero, which powered the *Gripens*. Their lead engineer would be Rune Hyrefeldt, head of Military Program management. While GKN's headquarters were located in Trollhätten, Sweden, they would be working out of their Military Program offices, conveniently co-located with SAAB in Linköping.

When the French *Rafale* was first envisioned in the late 1970s, it was seen as an aircraft that would replace and consolidate the fighter fleets of both the French Air Force and Navy. Its responsibilities would include air supremacy, interdiction, aerial reconnaissance, ground support, in-depth strike, anti-ship strike, and nuclear deterrence missions. Now the objective would be that the *Rafale's* successor be equal to or better than the Russian or Chinese fifth-generation fighters, the Sukhoi Su-57 and the Chengdu J-20.

The manufacturer of the next generation of French fighter aircraft would be the same as that of the *Rafale*; Aerospatiale, formerly Dassault Aviation. Their corporate headquarters were located in the city center of Paris. However, Aerospatiale was now a division of Airbus. And the Defense and Space division of Airbus, as noted above, was in Ottobrunn, Germany.

As for the Eurofighter *Typhoon's* successor, it would again be a collaboration of Airbus, BAE Systems, and Leonardo. As before, the Airbus segment of the work would be done in Ottobrunn, Germany. The headquarters for the operations of BAE which would be working on some of the components was located in Farnborough in England. As the offices were outside the purview of the European Union's 5G network, gaining access to the details of their work would be somewhat more difficult for the Chinese. Finally, the design and fabrication facilities of Leonardo which would be contributing components to the aircraft were headquartered in Rome. They developed and integrated systems for the control and protection of land and sea borders. They also developed secure communications networks and solutions for the management of infrastructure and systems. Their operations, headquartered in Rome, would be well within the scope of China's monitoring of the EU's 5G network and provide access to any innovations.

Chapter Thirteen

Having taken all the actions both available and
necessary to allow them to prevent the armed forces of the
nations of the European Union from gaining an upper hand
on their burgeoning military might, the Chinese had one
other geopolitical factor to take into consideration. Of the
27 member nations of the EU, 21 are members of NATO.
And its key doctrine, embodied in Article 5 of the treaty,
states "that an armed attack against one or more of them in
Europe or North America shall be considered an attack
against them. . .", meaning all the other members. That
meant any offensive action by China would be retaliated
against by the United States.

The Chinese had taken a beating in their previous
military encounter with the U.S. when they invaded Taiwan
in the Winter of 2021, but that engagement had proven that
the two countries could go to battle without the absolute
necessity of resorting to nuclear weapons. Nonetheless, that
eventuality always existed.

The next consideration was the updating of China's
Ministry of State Security, the country's foreign intelligence
agency, dossiers on each of the EU nations' heads of state.
The group was a heterogeneous mix. After the departure of
the United Kingdom, there were four Kings, one Queen, one
Grand Duke, and twenty-one Presidents. Each had his or

her own distinct protective detail which was composed of from state police all the way up to armies. China would have to penetrate each unit's ring of security around its protectee in order to fill in the well-protected gaps in each individual's political, health, and mental health profiles.

Direct access to the head of state under scrutiny was out of the question. And public revelations about them which appeared on broadcast television, public radio, or in print were usually both limited and screened by their press offices to cast them in their most favorable light. But the webcams which pervaded society would reveal images of them entering or leaving the offices of doctors, psychiatrists, or other practitioners, the visits to whom would give insights into the subject's weaknesses.

By combining the publicly-released profile of each head of state with the take from the widely-distributed webcams which, using facial recognition software, caught images of both male and female heads of state entering the homes or places of business of their colleagues, partners, and attendees revealed their less-than-public identities, the Chinese could use the implied frailties in character and indiscretions as leverage against their potential enemies.

And then, of course, there were the social media outlets. Facebook, Twitter, and Instagram could be used by the Chinese to cast discredit upon the character of any head of state by displaying their reclusive conduct to their constituents. Subtly, but pervasively, the Chinese would attempt to bring the character of each nation's leader into question in the minds of their subjects. The purpose would be to offer the Chinese leadership as a trustworthy and stable alternative to the present domestic head of state.

But social media had one more essential role to play in the Chinese government's plan. Because of its pervasive nature in society, the spin applied to the news stories presented had a subtle but effective impact upon how the citizens of the EU viewed the world around them. While attempting to detract from society's current institutions, social media also offered the opportunity to enhance the public's view of other alternatives. With the complicity of the social media giants, this tactic had been employed by the campaign of President Robert Allen and his Democrat colleagues against their Republican opponents in the 2020 election. And the effectiveness with which they employed it had not been lost on the Chinese.

There were a number of policies and institutions which were, or had been, employed by many of the nations of the European Union which had fallen into disrepute. Reminding their citizens of their nation's history, even in a corrupt or inaccurate way, could cause the citizenry to think twice about their heritage. In doing so, they could cast a country's history in a less-than-benevolent light and cause the people to reexamine their heritage more critically. *The New York Times* had conducted just such an attempt with their 1619 Project through which they tried to convince Americans that their country's history and global supremacy did not begin in 1776 with the American Revolution against Great Britain but with the arrival of slaves from Africa in 1619.

In a similar manner, the Chinese resurrected stories of the colonial histories of many of the EU's members. A good number of them had established colonies in Africa, South America, Asia, and throughout the world. In 1960, the United Nations had adopted Resolution 1514, entitled *Declaration on the Granting of Independence to Colonial Countries and Peoples*. It characterized foreign rule as a violation of human rights, affirmed the right to self-determination, and called for an end to colonial rule.

As Adom Getachew wrote, "Within fifteen years, anticolonial nationalists had successfully captured the UN and transformed the General Assembly into a platform for the international politics of decolonization." During the vote on the adoption of the resolution, 89 countries voted for it, none voted against it, and nine abstained. Eight of those nine had been the world's greatest colonial powers and included Belgium, France, Portugal, and Spain, as well as the United Kingdom and the United States.

Many Europeans were not well-versed in their own country's colonial past and found it all rather distasteful. Taken one step further, it was not difficult to delude the masses through strategically-placed posts in social media into believing that if their own countries could have carried out such "atrocities", what were they up to now? The posts, of course, were being submitted by the Communist Party of China.

Had the posts openly come from such an obvious source as China, the administrators and dubiously entitled "fact-checkers" could have simply deleted the submitter's accounts and blocked any further attempts at subterfuge and the undermining of the legitimacy of the ruling governments of the European Union. But China had a solution. They established dummy ISPs, or Internet Service Providers, and submitted their posts using their IP (Internet Protocol) account numbers in such a way that they could not be easily traced.

Day in and day out, the residents of the European Union were being subliminally barraged with social media posts that were taking incremental bits of their national identity away from them. What was not being exposed were the colonial quests of the Communist Party of China and its precursor regimes themselves. It was part of China's legacy that they saw the entire world as subject to their conquest.

There were two contemporary examples of their never-ending quest for expansion. The first was the case of Taiwan, officially the Republic of China. The Chinese representation that Taiwan was nothing more than a "rogue province" which had broken off from mainland China was a gross misrepresentation of reality. Mao Zedong and his Communist troops had driven the Kuomintang led by Chiang Kai-shek, the legitimate government of China, off the mainland and onto a 14,000-square-mile island across the 81-mile-wide Taiwan Strait. Ever since 1949, the Communist Party of China had been trying to bring Taiwan back into the fold. In 2021 it had invaded the island which, with the assistance of the United States, had beat them back.

And then there was Hong Kong founded in 214 AD. In 1842 it had become a British Crown Colony under the Treaty of Nanking which ended England's First Opium War with China. The Sino-British Joint Declaration signed on December 19th, 1984, called for the return of Hong Kong to China on July 1st, 1997.

In accordance with the "one country, two systems" principle agreed to between the United Kingdom and China, the Hong Kong Special Administrative Region would not be required to practice the same socialist governmental system which ruled mainland China. Rather Hong Kong would be permitted to continue operating under its existing capitalist system and way of life for 50 years until 2047. That Joint Declaration required that those policies be written into the Hong Kong Basic Law. But in 2019 and 2020, Hong Kong residents participated in the Anti-Extradition Law Amendment Bill Movement. China responded by ringing the former colony with People's Liberation Army troops.

Chapter Fourteen

China's agenda of subverting the military, economic, and political underpinnings of the European Union continued across the continent for the remainder of 2021 and throughout 2022. Boris Johnson had had both the opportunity and the potential to become the first European leader since Maggie Thatcher, the "Iron Lady", in the 1980s to unify Europe. And although the United Kingdom had withdrawn from the European Union, the U.K. still exerted a disproportionate influence over European life and economics. But Johnson had gone soft on Communism, principally at the implied request and in response to the explicit influences of America's Allen Administration.

Angela Merkel had been the *de facto* leader of the European Union since coming to power as the Chancellor of Germany in 2005, but she had not sought a fifth term as chancellor in 2021. In October 2018, Merkel announced that she would not seek reelection as leader of Christian Democratic Union (CDU), Germany's ruling party, when they met in December 2018, but that she intended to remain as chancellor until the German federal election in 2021. Further, she indicated that she would seek no further political office.

While she chose not to suggest any person as her successor as leader of the CDU, political observers had long considered Annegret Kramp-Karrenbauer to be Merkel's protégé groomed for succession. This assumption was validated when Kramp-Karrenbauer was elected to succeed Merkel as leader of the CDU in December 2018. Her promotion to Defense Minister further solidified her status as the CDU's candidate and Merkel's successor. In February 2020, Kramp-Karrenbauer announced that she would resign as party leader of the CDU in the Summer. She was succeeded by Armin Laschet, Minister/President of North Rhine – Westphalia, in the 2021 CDU leadership election.

Unfortunately, Laschet had adopted a lenient position with respect to Vladimir Putin and the Russian Federation. He was against "demonizing" Putin for the Russian annexation of Crimea. He had also expressed a desire for a closer relationship with China. Finally, he was outspoken against the prospect of excluding Huawei from bidding on the development of the European Union's 5G network. It appeared that if there was to be an EU "strongman", it would have to come from somewhere other than Germany.

As unlikely as it may have seemed, the new European Union strongman turned out to be yet another woman, Marion Anne Perrine (better known as "Marine") Le Pen. Following the assassination of French President Emmanuel Macron in Guatemala in October of 2017, his second-in-command, Gérard Larcher, the President of the French Senate, had been sworn in as Acting President. However, since the previous federal election had taken place less than a year earlier, a new election was called rather than have Larcher serve out the 4+ remaining years in Macron's term. Le Pen, the head of the conservative National Rally party, had easily defeated Larcher and would serve out the remainder of Macron's term until the next election in 2022.

The 48-year-old Marine Le Pen was a lawyer and politician who had served as the President of the National Rally, previously known as the National Front, since 2011. She was the youngest daughter of the former National Front leader Jean-Marie Le Pen and the aunt of former National Front Member of Parliament Marion Maréchal. Le Pen had joined the National Front as far back as 1986.

Le Pen had won the leadership of the National Front in 2011 with 67.6% of the vote, defeating Bruno Gollnisch and succeeding her father who had been president of the party since he founded it in 1972. In 2012, she had placed third in the federal presidential election collecting 17.9% of the vote behind François Holland and Nicolas Sarkozy. She then ramped up a second presidential campaign for 2017. She finished second in the first round of the election with 21.3% of the vote and faced Emmanuel Macron of the centrist *En Marche!* party in the second round. On May 7th, 2017, she conceded after receiving approximately 33.9% of the vote. Following Macron's assassination, Le Pen announced her candidacy and defeated former State Senator Larcher, winning two-thirds of the vote.

Upon her election, the 48-year-old President Le Pen exhibited more moderate policies than her nationalist father had espoused. She endorsed a movement of "de-demonization of the National Front" in an effort to make the party's image more palatable to a larger segment of the population. More controversial members of the party were expelled for showing both racism and antisemitism. She even expelled her own father from the party in 2015 for making controversial statements. She made it clear that she would act upon her opposition to both NATO and the United States and pledged to withdraw France from both of their spheres of influence. Finally, upon her re-election in 2022, she announced that she would make public a new agenda of initiatives with respect to the future of the European Union after the German elections were held in September.

In spite of the dominance of Merkel and Le Pen in the routine dealings of governments, it could not be claimed that the European Union had no "strongmen" in the traditional sense of the word. Several of the heads of state from the former Eastern Bloc countries which were now members of the EU could be characterized as strongmen. But they were thugs. In the 1980s, leaders like Reagan and Thatcher were strongmen, but they ruled and influenced by their wits, not by force. Of course, there was always the military might to back them up. But, more often than not, it was held in reserve as an implied threat.

The Chinese were not oblivious to the ascendancy of

Le Pen as Merkel's successor. While her popularity tended to fluctuate throughout her first term in office, it had rebounded solidly in 2020 based upon her handling of the Covid-19 pandemic. In the 2022 federal election, no other candidate posed a credible threat to Le Pen's charisma.

Although Germany had always been the economic powerhouse after the United Kingdom in the European Union before its withdrawal under Brexit, Merkel's immigration policy had eroded its supremacy and Le Pen's economic policies had placed France in the lead position. She had prepared France for prosperity in her second term.

As 2022 rolled to a close with the arrival of the traditional religious gift-giving holidays, Christians and Jews throughout the European Union were searching for that perfect gift. Less than eighteen months earlier, at the conclusion of a G-7 (Group of Seven industrialized nations, formed by Canada, France, Germany, Italy, Japan, the United Kingdom, and the United States) Summit, a communiqué was issued on economy and trade. "With regard to China," it began, "and competition in the global economy, we will *continue to consult* on collective approaches to challenging non-market policies and practices which undermine the fair and transparent operation of the global economy." Beijing responded, accusing the West of "slandering" China's "peaceful development" and bringing back a "Cold War mentality."

And yet the Chinese had already devised an agenda of their own. Moreso than at any other time of the year, people were flocking to the social media outlets such as Facebook seeking the best deals on the most popular gifts. And they were finding prices which were significantly lower than those which prevailed at their local retailers. By clicking on "Shop now", they were taken to the website of a no-name retailer where they could purchase the item by doing nothing more than entering their credit card data.

Unless the shopper had chosen a little-known feature on their credit card account which called for them to receive an email or text message alert whenever a purchase was made from a retailer with corporate offices outside their home country, the first they would know that the payment would be going a company in China would be when they opened their credit card bill in January, long after the gift had been presented to the recipient.

And the deceptive trade practices did not stop there. Online retailers such as Amazon.com and ebay, which made a practice of selling used and highly discounted items, were being used by China to market their goods in the West. When the seller knew that the item was coming from China, they put a comment in the description section to that effect. The item always listed the location from which it would ostensibly be shipped. But in numerous cases, that location was nothing more than a dummy domestic corporation with a warehouse in one of the commercial centers of China.

Chapter Fifteen

While Chinese retailers and knockoffs predominated the 2022 holiday season, Chinese entrepreneurs had been keeping a close eye on the retail markets in the West and had learned their lessons well. Whatever the Western businesses could sell to the public, the Chinese could sell at a cheaper price and in greater volume. The epitome of China's businessmen and their models are represented by Jack Ma and Jeff Bezos.

In 1994, Jeff Bezos, then 30, founded what would become Amazon, America's premier retailer. Amazon is a multinational technology company focusing on e-commerce, cloud computing, and artificial intelligence. In information technology (IT), it is one of the Big Five along with Google, Apple, Microsoft, and Facebook. It is referred to as "one of the most influential economic and cultural forces in the world." While it started as an online retailer for books, it soon moved into electronics, software, apparel, jewelry, and food. In 2015 it surpassed Walmart as the most valuable retailer in the United States by market capitalization.

Amazon has a publishing arm, a film and television studio, and a cloud computing subsidiary, Amazon Web Services (AWS), which markets its products to everyone from other corporations to government agencies including the Central Intelligence Agency (CIA). They even manufactured some of their own consumer electronics products including the omnipresent Kindle e-readers. If Americans or, for that matter, Canadians, Japanese, Italians, Germans, or any other nationality wanted to buy it, Amazon or one of its associated vendors were happy to supply it.

In Hangzhou, China, Jeff Bezos had a disciple. Only one year Bezos' junior, Jack Ma, a degree from Hangzhou Normal University in hand, was in search of a business in which he could apply his degree and ambition. Six years after receiving his degree, Jack Ma became aware of the internet and an idea was born.

His company derived its name from Ali Baba, one of the characters from the Middle Eastern folk-tale collection *One Thousand and One Arabian Nights*. Jack Ma felt that the name had universal appeal. As he tells the story:

"One day I was in San Francisco in a coffee shop, and I was thinking Alibaba is a good name. And then a waitress came, and I said, *'Do you know about Alibaba?'* And she said *'Yes'*. I said, *'What do you know about him?'*, and she said *'Open Sesame'*. And I said, *'Yes, this is the name!'* Then I went on to the street and found 30 people and asked them, *'Do you know Alibaba?'* People from India, people from Germany, and people from Tokyo and China . . . they all knew about Alibaba. Alibaba – open sesame. Alibaba is a kind, smart business person, and he helped the village. So . . . easy to spell, and globally known. Alibaba opens sesame for small- to medium-sized companies."

On June 28ᵗʰ, 1999, Jack Ma and 17 of his friends and students founded Alibaba.com, a China-based B2B (business-to-business) marketplace site, in his Hangzhou apartment. Alibaba.com was expected to improve the domestic e-commerce market and perfect an e-commerce platform for Chinese enterprises, especially small- and medium-sized enterprises, to help export Chinese products to the global market. In 2002, Alibaba.com became profitable three years after its launch.

In 2010, Jack Ma founded the Amazon.com clone, transaction-based retail website AliExpress.com, which allows smaller buyers to buy small quantities of goods at wholesale prices. Any consumer from the West can go on AliExpress and find anything from electronics gear to automotive accessories to apparel at prices that are from 25 to 50% less than in their local store or even Amazon.com. Moreover, due to their vendors' use of state-sponsored shipping services, the cost to get an item halfway around the world ranges from free to a nominal charge. And if there's a problem with the item, be it not as described or defective, the vendor simply lets the customer keep it rather than require that they return it at the exorbitant prices charged by American shipping services for which they would bear the burden. And then they send a replacement at no charge.

So now there were two contingents of shoppers who

were patronizing China's retailers and bolstering the PRC's economy at the expense of the European Union's businesses. The first was the shoppers who were simply buying from retailers who they believed were domestic because the Chinese had set up a dummy corporation in their country but were actually based in and shipping from China. The second were those who were knowingly shopping at institutions in China because there were no domestic businesses that could sell the items in demand for the prices they could be had for from China.

But then there were the more unwittingly and less culpable shoppers who were also helping to enrich the Chinese economy at the expense of either their home country's economy or that of an ally. An excellent example was automobile tires. Of course, people knew that BMWs and Mercedes came from Germany. Hyundais and KIAs came from South Korea. But a key component, tires, was being farmed out.

The Chinese tire industry, which had grown exponentially for more than a decade, was profiting from Western purchases. Chinese tire production had been putting in steady numbers year after year. The 2015 acquisition of Italian tiremaker Pirelli by China's ChemChina and the recent bid by another Chinese tire producer to acquire South Korean heavyweight Kumho Tire Company has catapulted Chinese producers to the big leagues. Catered by an estimated 230 large and small tiremakers, the Chinese tire industry has surprised the global tire industry with its unprecedented growth. Currently, China is the world's largest market for tires. The Chinese automobile industry has grown at a tremendous pace. This has catalyzed the development of the country's tire sector, both in terms of production as well as consumption.

Most of the mid-scale Chinese tiremakers operate on very low margins, thus even a marginal change in raw material prices plays havoc with their survival. After four years of oversupply of natural rubber and low oil prices, the main ingredients of synthetic rubber, these costs are rising. Since these costs account for about 60% of total input costs for a number of Chinese tiremakers, most of them would be forced to increase their prices in the coming months, eventually eroding their price advantage in domestic and export markets.

Several top global brands such as Michelin (two production plants), Bridgestone (six plants), Goodyear (two plants), Continental (two plants), Pirelli (two plants), Yokohama (three plants), Hankook (four plants), and Kumho (three plants) are present in China through their manufacturing units. In 2016, China exported tires worth $12.89 billion to more than 200 countries. The U.S. remained the largest export market. The value of tires exported from China to the U.S. was $2.1 billion, accounting for 16.3% of China's total export value of tires.

With exports worth $541 million, the U.K. was the second-largest market, accounting for 4.2% of China's total export value of tires. Zhongce Rubber Group (also known as ZC Rubber) remains the No. 1 tire manufacturer in China in terms of yearly sales, with 2016 sales of 18.38 billion yuan. In second place, Giti Tire trails by more than 6 billion yuan, with annual revenues of 13.14 billion yuan in 2016. Third place Sailun Jinyu Group had a reported income of 11.19 billion yuan. Doublestar, which has recently made a bid for a majority stake in Kumho Tire, is at sixth position with 2016 sales of 7.26 billion yuan.

Amid the fast-growing Chinese automobile market, the world's major tire giants have deployed production bases in China and further increased investment in expansion in the last two years. In November 2016, Goodyear broke ground on a $485 million expansion of its state-of-the-art tire facility in Pulandian located in Dalian province. Upon completion in 2020, the expansion increased the plant's capacity by about 5 million tires a year, enabling Goodyear to meet the growing market demand for premium, large-rim-diameter consumer tires in China. Goodyear was the first global tire manufacturer to enter China when it invested in a tire manufacturing plant in Dalian in 1994. The company moved production to the new Pulandian factory in 2012. Another global giant, Continental, started its Phase III project at its Hefei-based production facility in November 2015 to increase its installed capacity in China to 14 million tires per annum.

Besides acquisitions, Chinese tiremakers are also setting up their manufacturing units in a number of countries. Chinese tire companies have opted for these investments due to intense competition in the domestic market and anti-dumping duties imposed on imports of China-produced tires by a number of countries. Southeast Asia is the most preferred destination of Chinese tiremakers due to the ample availability of natural rubber, comparative labor costs, and proximity to China. For instance, China's largest tire producer, Hangzhou Zhongce Rubber, has built a new facility in Thailand. Other major tire producers from the country, such as Linglong Tire, Sentaida, and Double Coin have also established a manufacturing presence in Thailand to capitalize on the robust automotive market of the country. Qingdao FullRun Tyre Corp. Ltd. is investing $200 million to set up a factory in Malaysia. The Chinese company signed a memorandum of understanding with the Port Klang Free Trade Zone (PKFTZ) in December 2016.

Thus, it was apparent that purchases made in an allied country could well be benefiting the bottom line of the People's Republic of China. The Chinese had insinuated their production capacity into virtually every aspect of the world's industrial output. It would take an all-out effort on the part of the West to deny China the benefit from the world's rebound from the depression caused by the Covid-19 pandemic.

There were numerous other Chinese products that contributed to the nation's bottom line. One of them was the computer chips manufactured using rare earth metals upon which China had seemed to have cornered the market. Rare earth metals are components of every computer chip.

China has dominated rare earths production for a number of years. In 2020, its domestic output of 140,000 metric tons was up from 132,000 metric tons the previous year. Chinese producers must adhere to a quota system for rare earths production. The half-year quota for rare earth mining in 2021 had been set at 84,000 metric tons (up 27.2 percent from 2020), while the quota for smelting and separation was currently 81,000 tons (up 27.6 percent from 2020). Interestingly, this system led China to become the world's top importer of rare earths in 2018.

The quota system was a response to China's longstanding problems with illegal rare earths mining. Over the last decade, the country had taken steps to clean up its act, including shutting illegal or environmentally non-compliant rare earth mines and limiting production and rare earth exports.

Currently, six state-owned miners are in charge of China's rare earth industry, in theory allowing China to keep a strong handle on production. However, illegal rare earth extraction remains a challenge. The Chinese government has continually taken steps to help curb this activity.

Chapter Sixteen

As 2023 dawned, by use of its Chinese-built 5G internet and telecom network in the European Union, China had succeeded in retaining its military superiority over the EU. It had also attained a significant impact on the EU's economy. The final goal was to obtain substantive influence over the politics and ideology of the citizens of the EU nations and their governments. This last objective would require the exercise of a great degree of subtlety.

There was a certain irony to the approach which the Chinese would have to employ in their efforts to undermine capitalist governments in favor of more Left-Leaning ones which were subject to conversion, or overthrow, to socialism or Communism. The last countries to be admitted to the European Union were former members of the Eastern Bloc which was dominated by the Soviet Union. They included Bulgaria, Poland, the Czech Republic (formerly Czechoslovakia), Romania, and Hungary. Even Ukraine was teetering on the brink of joining the EU.

All of these countries had lived under Communism or a strict form of socialism until the fall of the Berlin Wall in 1989 and the dissolution of the Soviet Union in 1991. Consequently, they would exhibit a certain skepticism toward any subliminal campaigns on social media or reluctance to fall prey to their implied promises. Some

Western European countries, on the other hand, had had their share of active Communist parties for nearly a century. Their popularity had ebbed and flowed, but there was still a core constituency whether formally recognized as a political party or not. It was they who would be the prime target of Chinese propaganda in the short run.

The Communist parties of France, Italy, Spain, Portugal, and Ireland were still in existence. Membership in these parties had been all the rage during portions of the 1970s and '80s. Ideologies were passed on from generation to generation and by 2023 the children and grandchildren of those comrades could still be found though some were more open or active in their practice of the political ideals of Communism than others. Nonetheless, there was a core.

Those feeling disenfranchised by the predominant party in a country are always the most susceptible to an alternative group espousing a Utopian ideology. But the way China would have to go about "recruitment" of those seeking a different sort of government or alliance, which is what the European Union was, would have to be courted seductively. And their allegiance to their own country's bureaucracy would have to be challenged before a system consistent with the Communist Party of China's ideology could be offered as the desirable alternative.

The most effective way to plant alternative ideas in the mind of a subject was to present the compelling news of the day or controversial political offensives and then present, in a low-key manner, other ways of viewing or interpreting the same set of accepted facts. The more one was dissatisfied with the *status quo*, the more likely they were to be seduced by an alternative theory or resolution.

China had great plans for the European Union, but, over the millennia, they had learned patience. They had also learned that great endeavors often started with seemingly small, insignificant steps. Thus would be the case of their assault on the European Union. Their first initiative would be focused on one of Europe's smallest targets; Gibraltar.

In June 2016, the United Kingdom conducted a vote as to whether or not to remain in the European Union. Gibraltar, a British Overseas Territory, was a part of the U.K. and its economy was nearly totally dependent on the EU as it was completely encompassed by its members, the Mediterranean Sea, and the Atlantic Ocean. That fact was not lost on Spain or the PCE, the Communist Party of Spain.

For the purposes of the Maastricht Treaty which provided for the underpinnings of the European Union, Gibraltar was a member of the EU by virtue of its British Overseas Territory status, although it was clearly entirely dependent upon the United Kingdom in matters of foreign relations and defense. And there were unique treaties signed between the two governing economic matters. On November 7th, 2002, Gibraltar held a referendum on

sovereignty. By a vote of 17,900, or 98.97%, to 187, or
1.03%, the Gibraltarians voted against shared sovereignty
under both Great Britain and Spain. The citizens' desire to
remain British was overwhelming. However, in the June
23rd, 2016, referendum on Brexit, on whether to remain in
the European Union or leave, the citizens of Gibraltar voted
19,322, or 95.91% to remain, while only 823, or 4.09%,
expressed a desire to leave. This was in stark contrast to the
51.89% vs. 48.11% result to leave in the United Kingdom as
a whole.

In response to the United Kingdom's Prime Minister
Theresa May's triggering of Article 50 of the charter of the
European Union on March 29th, 2019, the EU released a
summary of its agenda for the withdrawal negotiations. One
stated objective was a definitive determination of the status
of Gibraltar within the EU and included a possible extension
to Spain of a right to veto Gibraltar's future trade relations
with EU member nations. This raised the hackles of a
number of British politicians, both active and retired.

Members of the House of Commons were quick to
brand such a provision as "utterly unacceptable". A former
leader of the U.K.'s Conservative Party, Michael Howard,
stated that Theresa May should be prepared to go to war to
defend Gibraltar just as Maggie Thatcher had done with
Argentina over the Falklands 35 years previous. These
words came close on the heels of an interview given by
Defense Secretary Sir Michael Fallon on April 2nd wherein

he said, "Gibraltar is going to be protected all the way because the sovereignty of Gibraltar cannot be changed without the agreement of the people of Gibraltar, and they have made it very clear they do not want to live under Spanish rule."

The following day Spain's Foreign Minister, Alfonso Dastis, said that the entire issue was being blown all out of proportion. "The Spanish government is a little surprised by the tone of comments coming out of Britain, a country known for its composure," said Dastis at a conference in Madrid. For his part, Gibraltar's Chief Minister, Fabian Picardo, chastised EU Council President Donald Tusk for presuming to give Spain a right of veto in any future negotiations between Gibraltar and EU member nations.

"Mr. Tusk, who has been given to using the analogies of the divorce and divorce petition," said Picardo, "is behaving like a cuckolded husband who is taking it out on the children." Picardo made it clear that Spain was trying to bully Gibraltar, and that the EU was allowing the bullying to take place. He said that Gibraltar would not allow itself to become a bargaining chip in the Brexit negotiations.

"We are not going to be a chip and we are not going to be a victim of Brexit," continued Picardo, "as we are not the culprits of Brexit: we voted to stay in the European Union, so taking it out on us is to allow Spain to behave in the manner of the bully." He insisted that the EU should remove any references to Gibraltar from its negotiating guidelines. "Removal of the reference to Gibraltar," he concluded, "would be a sign of good faith and goodwill."

It was here that the influence of the Communist Party of Spain began to subtly inject itself into the political agenda and dialog. As the United Kingdom had withdrawn from the European Union, the financial prosperity of Gibraltar had, for the moment, been extracted from the Iberian Peninsula. But there had been subtle gestures by the PCE to influence the ultimate outcome of the Brexit agreement.

The district of Spain immediately adjacent to Gibraltar had little in the way of an economic base. What prosperity it enjoyed was derived from the incomes of the Spaniards who daily traveled the causeway to Gibraltar to work in its banking industry, tourist attractions, or gambling institutions. It took little effort on the part of the PCE to motivate the locals to lobby their politicians to hold out for a say in any of Gibraltar's future economic undertakings.

The lobbying had been gently "encouraged" by the seemingly well-intentioned observations in the Spanish-language posts in the EU's social media. The PCE had placed them there using dummy social media "groups" at the "suggestion" of the Communist Party of China. At the opposite end of the EU in the East, a different dynamic was taking place. The previous members of the Eastern Bloc would require a different set of motivators for reform.

The Digital Silk Road

Chapter Seventeen

As long ago as the early days of Lech Wałęsa and the Solidarity movement in Gdańsk, Poland in 1980, the "masses", supposedly the beneficiaries of the fruits of Communism, had begun to revolt against their masters. Wałęsa, an electrician at the Lenin Shipyard who became a trade union activist, eventually found himself the leader of a 10-million-member trade union and ultimately the President of Poland in 1990. His election took place in the midst of the period from 1989 which marked the fall of the Berlin Wall to 1991 which saw the dissolution of the Soviet Union.

The collapse of the Eastern Bloc followed logically when its ideological model, the Soviet Union, ceased to exist. Each of the five nations which joined the European Union was now lead by an individual invested with the title of President. And these five individuals were chosen in what were ostensibly "free elections".

The published results of these elections were frequently the butt of numerous jokes or blasphemous editorials, but the results stood and the person selected took office. However, in former Communist countries, free elections did not guarantee democracy. And the hierarchy did not resemble what the American Constitution set forth as a table of organization for any contemporary democracy.

Governments formerly in the sphere of influence of the Soviet Union derived their revenue, what little there was of it, from state-owned industries. By the process of natural selection, a group of men emerged who were, by far, the best at running large companies. They were, to use Western terminology, the "captains of industry". To use the literal term, they were "oligarchs".

The dictionary defines an oligarch as "a person who belongs to a small group of people who govern or control a country, business, etc." In the case of the Russian Federation, the former Communist countries now in the European Union, and many of the former Soviet republics, the role of the oligarch fulfilled all of the possibilities in the definition. In reality, they were all oligarchies.

The oligarchs were awarded the honor of managing a state-owned business with the reasonable expectation that they would turn a significant profit. In the event that they did so, they were handsomely rewarded by the state. And, because the economy of the nation and the revenues which it had to spend to keep the nation afloat was totally dependent upon these oligarchs, the "President" was obliged to keep them happy by governing the country in compliance with their wishes. In reality, the President worked for the oligarchs and not *vice versa* as one might have assumed.

Consequently, the Western nation of Spain was being governed, if only by leverage, by the Communists while the

Eastern nations were being ruled by the Communist-oriented oligarchs. The Communist Party of China seemed to have the Eastern and Western extremes of the European Union already under the direct influence of Communist ideology. It was now time to go to work on the heart. That meant Germany and France.

In 2015, Germany's Chancellor Angela Merkel, then recognized as the preeminent head of state in the European Union, made a fateful and fatal decision. A flood of refugees had been crossing Syria and the intervening countries on their way to Europe in an effort to escape the deadly regime of Syria's Bashar al-Assad. Along the way, those fleeing had been joined by others in addition to the Syrian rebels themselves. Some were of other nationalities and some were soldiers from the Islamic State in Syria (ISIS). The mass of humanity in flight had been characterized as a humanitarian crisis.

In August 2015, Merkel issued a proclamation that refugees from Syria would be allowed to submit asylum applications if they reached Germany after having passed through the intervening European Union countries. Subsequently, 1.1 million asylum seekers entered Germany. Germans' opposition to the government's admission policy with respect to the new wave of immigrants was both negative and virulent, accompanied by unruly anti-immigration protests.

It was Merkel's contention that the German economy was robust enough to withstand the drastic influx of immigrants and she repeated that there would be no limit to the number of refugees and immigrants that Germany would accept. In September 2015, pro-immigration demonstrators across the country warmly welcomed the arriving refugees and immigrants. Horst Seehofer, the head of the sister party to Merkel's Christian Democratic Union (CDU), the Christian Social Union in Bavaria (CSU), and Bavarian Minister-President, expressed his objection to Merkel's decision. He said that the immigrants were "in a state of mind without rules, without system, and without order because of a German decision."

As it turned out, 30% of the supposed asylum seekers reaching the German border were, in actuality, from other countries. Nonetheless, Yasmin Fahimi, Secretary-General of the Social Democratic Party (SPD) and junior partner of the ruling coalition, praised Merkel's policy of allowing immigrants in Hungary to enter Germany as "a strong signal of humanity to show that Europe's values are valid also in difficult times."

In November 2015, discussions took place among the members of the ruling coalition to prevent any further family unification for immigrants for two years, and to create "Transit Zones" on the German border and, for immigrants with a low likelihood of having their asylum applications approved, to be sequestered there until their application was acted upon. The issue illustrated the conflict between the CSU which supported the policy and the SPD which opposed it. Merkel agreed to the adoption of the policy. But the ISIS attacks in Paris in November 2015 caused the necessity for the German government to reevaluate its stance on the European Union's policy toward immigrants.

It was apparent that there was a consensus among German government officials, with the exception of Merkel, that a higher level of scrutiny was needed in vetting immigrants with respect to their admission to Germany. However, while not officially limiting the influx numerically, Merkel tightened asylum policy in Germany.

In October 2016, Merkel had made a diplomatic trip to Mali and Niger in Africa. Her mission was to negotiate how their respective governments could remedy the conditions which were causing people from Africa to flee their home countries to seek illegal immigration to the European Union and, more specifically, to Germany. The immigration crisis had fostered conservative electoral preferences throughout Germany resulting in the Alternative for Germany (AfD) party garnering 12% of the vote in the 2017 federal election.

These developments demanded serious ideological debates over the causes for a marked increase in the Right-Wing populism emerging in Germany. Academics hypothesized that the increase in conservative preferences was the direct result of the German immigration crisis which had introduced nearly half a million people, predominantly Muslims, into the country. Germans were a relatively homogeneous nationality predominantly White and Christian. The loosening of immigration requirements had caused a nationwide perception that the change in policy had caused an ethnic and cultural threat to German society.

It was this result, and not its cause, upon which the Communist Party of China pounced. The Chinese were both ethnocentric and xenophobic. Their society welcomed neither non-Chinese races nor cultures. It was this similarity with German society on which the CPC would capitalize to entice the disaffected segment of the German population, which constituted a majority, to change their view of their ruling class.

Germany's federal election in 2021 marked the end of the Merkel regime and, with it, her immigration policies. The cost of the unemployment benefits and social welfare programs which had drained the country's coffers to support the immigrants who had made little contribution to the nation's economy had also threatened the sustainability of those programs to support the neediest of native Germans. In 2019, Jörg Meuthen was the leading candidate of the AfD in the European Parliament election. In March 2021, courts blocked the surveillance of the AfD as extremists to give all political parties an equal opportunity. That Fall, Alice Weidel, leader of the AfD, won the German federal election.

Chapter Eighteen

By January 2023, France and Germany had established themselves as the two preeminent economic powerhouses in the European Union. Moreover, French President Marine Le Pen and German Chancellor Alice Weidel were clearly the two most vibrant heads of state. While Weidel had carried on Angela Merkel's policies with the exception of her immigration agenda, Le Pen had done all in her power to stand Emmanuel Macron's policies on their heads.

President Macron had been a New Age World sort of guy. But just as President John Jefferson had been an "America First" style of leader, President Le Pen was a "France First" head of state. No Colonialist she. In America, in recent memory, the electorate had been roughly 40% Liberal and 40% Conservative with the 20% moderate and uncommitted in the middle deciding the outcome of national elections. In the Twenty-first century, France had started out being divided about 45% Nationalist and 45% Globalist with the 10% in the middle holding sway.

But that had all changed following the November 2015 Paris ISIS bomb attacks. The country was now divided more or less 65% Nationalist and 25% Globalist with that remaining 10% still undecided. Le Pen's Nationalism had stood her in good stead with the majority of the electorate.

In the realm of economics, Le Pen practiced protectionism and favored it over free trade. She called for the separation between the practices of investment and retail banking. And she promoted diversification within the energy generation industry.

Le Pen had been opposed to what was referred to as the "supranationalization of the European Union" as well as the use of the Euro as currency. She did, however, shift her position on those two issues as of 2019. Nonetheless, she recognized that multiculturalism within the European Union had failed. And she called for the "de-Islamification" of French society and a moratorium on legal immigration. She believed that the welfare benefits and social services available to immigrants served as an incentive for illegal immigration.

For the past several years, ever since the Chinese had commenced construction of the EU's 5G network, they had been closely observing the evolution of its leadership. The administrations of Le Pen and Weidel would be difficult institutions to overthrow, but they had time on their side. And the growing popularity of social media in that interval had only worked in their favor.

The strategy in Beijing was that it would insert "media viruses" into European life by way of the internet which would become self-sustaining and self-replicating. These would alter mass consciousness, especially among certain susceptible groups. The underlying philosophy was that if enough of those EU citizens who currently supported the capitalist economies of the European nations could be made to question capitalism's superiority as an ideology over Communism, then they would become ripe for socialist indoctrination.

Other than a person's family life, there were three fundamental determinants that contributed to an individual's sense of well-being. The first was prosperity. To the extent that a nation's economy was thriving, people believed that they were well-off and that their standard of living was secure. The second was their belief that their value system was reflected in the form and actions of their government. As long as they supported the day-to-day functioning of the government, they felt both heard and valued. And then there was safety. If it was their sense that their nation's military could protect them from attack or invasion, they felt they could go about life as they so chose. It was these three perceptions which the Chinese would challenge.

As noted previously, nations at the Western and Eastern extremes of the EU like Spain and the former Eastern Bloc countries were the most susceptible. It would be France and Germany that would be the hardest nuts to crack. From outside, they both appeared rock solid. But there were always seams in every rock. They just needed to be struck at the proper angle.

European analysts and intelligence operatives in China had spent years studying the policies of Marine Le Pen and Alice Weidel searching for positions and policies which could be used as points of weakness to be attacked in social media to help promote socialist and Communist causes.

President Le Pen's National Rally party had been embarrassed in a number of regional elections after several candidates were exposed as having made racist or other inappropriate comments prior to the 2021 elections. Its leading candidate in the Eastern Bourgogne-Franche-Comte region had been condemned after joking about farmer suicides. Julien Odoul was reported to have asked if a farmer who hung himself had used a French-made rope. Although he claimed his comment had been taken out of context, he did not deny having made it.

National Rally withdrew its support of their candidate in the 2021 election in the western Gironde region, Marta Le Nair, after previous anti-Semitic posts on social media were brought to light by the opposition. In 2015, Le Nair had said that after shaking hands with a Jew "you should check that you still have 10 fingers." A candidate in the central Creuse region was convicted of domestic violence and a second in the Ardennes was found to have a past conviction for child sex offenses. All these incidents came amidst Le Pen's campaign to "detoxify" her party after having taken it over from her father in 2011. Nonetheless, her political rivals were targeting her close advisors and junior party members for their racism and anti-Semitism.

As for Alice Weidel in Germany, her continuation of Chancellor Merkel's revised immigration policies had strengthened her country both economically and socially. Her administration's tone was clearly capitalist. Much of the economic resurgence had derived from the decreased demand on the welfare benefits and social services programs required by the un- and under-employed Syrian refugees as well as the immigrants who had accompanied them. Socially, the predominantly Muslim influx had torn the uniformly Teutonic culture asunder. One of Merkel's final actions during her tenure as chancellor, cutting back on immigration, had saved Germany from plummeting off a precarious economic cliff.

German administrations since the Cold War had ceased had proceeded upon the assumption that democracy had scored a permanent moral triumph rather than only a transient strategic victory that required constant vigilance. A unified Germany had become an economic monolith that had drifted away from its Western liberators and was more than willing to conduct trade with anyone and everyone who could enhance its economic standing. The underlying ideology was premised upon its continued faith in what was called "convergence", the post-1989 theory that integration and cooperation eventually converted all states into democracies and market economies. Although Russia had invaded both Georgia and Ukraine, assassinated political opponents in England and Germany, and contributed to the genocide by Bashar al-Assad in Syria, a myopic optimism persisted that a more developed trade relationship with Moscow and Beijing might tend to moderate their behavior.

The Western establishment was doing its best to perpetuate the notion that global security would be enhanced by a state of mutual dependency. Western non-governmental organizations (NGOs) failed to realize that to work to strengthen one's allies' was one of the best ways to ensure their continued freedom.

Members of the European Union did not acknowledge that both Russia and China considered Europe to be well within their sphere of influence and not simply the seat, along with the U.S., of Western power. The opportunity for Russia and China rested in the relative disunity of the EU, and in the fact that it was losing, not gaining, members.

NATO had flourished in the past six years with its $140 billion increase in revenues thanks to the prodding by former President John Jefferson. But while government bureaucracies, legacy media outlets, and elite universities celebrated the 16 years of Merkel's leadership in Europe, NATO had drifted. It needed to be reoriented into not solely a U.S. - EU partnership but a wholly Western Alliance.

Chapter Nineteen

In February 2023, President Xi Jinping convened another of his periodic meetings of his brain trust on the EU's 5G operation. The two usual members, Ren Zhengfei, the founder and Chief Executive Officer of Huawei, and Hou Weigu, the leader of ZTE, were in attendance. But now that the operation's intermediate phase was underway, there were other integral members.

Since the principal state-sponsored hacking was being performed by the staff of Unit 61398 from their headquarters on Datong Road in Shanghai, their leadership had been invited. The unit's head was Colonel Feng Wei, a graduate of China's University of Science and Technology. And his Deputy was Lieutenant Colonel Zhao Li who had received his undergraduate degree from Cal Tech before attending the Chinese Naval Command and Staff College in Nanjing.

With the hardware moguls and the men who inserted the propaganda into the social media outlets in the European Union present, the only element left to be accounted for was the source of the propaganda itself. Since the writing of propaganda was a learned skill that had to be continually practiced, the undisputed professionals were the Chinese journalists and their editors. The best in the business in China worked for *The Global Times*, *The People's Daily*, and the Xinhua News Agency.

On a tour of state media outlets in 2016, Xi Jinping made it a point of emphasizing that "the media must have The Party as their family name." The most widely read publication in the country was *The Global Times*, a daily tabloid newspaper published by *The People's Daily* newspaper which fell under the auspices of the Communist Party of China. The *Times* had sarcastically, but not inaccurately, been referred to as "China's Fox News". Its adherence to the CPC party line was unwavering.

The Xinhua News Agency was the state-run press agency of the People's Republic of China. The President and Editor-in-Chief of Xinhua, He Ping, was a member of the Central Committee of the CPC. It had been accurately deemed "the world's biggest propaganda agency". Previously, the Central Propaganda Department of the party sent daily faxes to all media outlets with a list of acceptable and unacceptable subjects for coverage along with talking points. They subsequently transitioned to conference calls for the same purpose but without leaving any paper trail.

A former editor for *The People's Daily* had reported that the party, by holding the reins on "ideological domain, material means, and living necessities," coerced the editors and reporters to publish only that which served the state's interests. In 2020, *The Global Times* published a story in praise of China's handling of the Covid-19 pandemic. On June 11th, Twitter announced that China had deleted 170,000 accounts under the pretense that they were perpetuating false claims about the state's culpability in the spread of the virus with its source in the Wuhan Institute of Virology.

As the meeting got underway, President Xi led off with some remarks and observations on the current state of affairs in the United States.

"I find our current situation somewhat fascinating. I would have always believed that the last place that either socialism or Communism could take hold would be America. But the last fifteen years have proven me wrong. The social unrest and benign neglect by President Hayes' Democrat administration, along with his healthcare and social welfare programs, subliminally introduced the citizenry to some of the fundamental underpinnings of a socialist society. And then there was his tendency to ignore those elements of his policies which only fomented racial unrest.

"For the most part, if we disregard the incidents which were a result of attacks by ISIS, the current state of political and social affairs in the European Union is marginally more stable than that of the United States under President Allen's Administration. New social policies and the resurgence of racism have lead to a situation which seems, from afar, to be teetering on the brink. But we are not here to speak about America. It is now time to make our most intense onslaught in the realm of social media in Europe.

"He Ping, in your opinion what are the subjects our propaganda campaign should be focused upon, and where are the governments of the European Union most vulnerable?" asked President Xi. The President and Editor-in-Chief of the Xinhua News Agency took a few moments to contemplate his response before answering. He was well aware that whatever he said could determine the future of the European Union and, by extension, the Western world.

"I have been observing, with great interest, the development of the 5G network in the European Union by our colleagues from Huawei and ZTE. They have done an admirable job and I am well aware of the hardware and software 'backdoors' that have been installed to allow us to manipulate whatever data is transmitted within the system. It is that capability that has allowed the project to proceed to its next step.

"We have maximized our capability to monitor virtually every aspect of EU society and commercial operation. Be it the facial recognition software which can track any subject, be they a governmental official or a suspected intelligence operative, through every motion in their daily life by means of the omnipresent network of webcams to the development of the next generation of weaponry by tapping into the military contractors' security camera systems, no element of activity in the EU can escape our all-seeing eyes.

"As for social media, our dummy corporations and organizations have been freely able to insert posts which are supportive or conducive to the introduction of an increasing number of subliminal concepts which exhibit the acceptability, if not the superiority, of both socialism and Communism in the conduct of daily life. This will be of assistance in our getting the European public to expect certain behaviors on the part of their leaders and government officials. What comes next is the question which we, in this room, are charged with carrying out.

"I believe that those of us here have the ability to chart the course for the future of the European Union. At the most elemental level, we can simply manipulate the wills and desires of the populace and let those preferences and tendencies, over time, dictate their choices in everything from consumer goods to political leaders. That process could well take a long time and the changes it elicits will, at first, be only nominal.

"At a more advanced level, using the distinguished journalists and editors we have here with us in the room today and at our disposal, we could bring about political upheaval which would more rapidly result in changes in political behavior and preferred political parties. That would play into our hands as the next generation of political leaders would have to be more receptive to the basic tenets of socialism and Communism than those of capitalism. They would be more inclined, if not compelled, to accept Chinese manufacturers' goods which would bring in European capital while, at the same time, adopting the practices and methods of our own means of production to produce goods domestically. The common man would be required to accept those values if they wished to continue to work in the EU economy.

"Finally, in the long term, if, by means of censorship and the introduction of increasingly seductive propaganda, our influence upon what did and did not flow through the 5G network could render the European Union vulnerable to subtle takeover by subversive elements of the Chinese state. Not a shot would need to be fired. The invasion would be subliminal and cultural, but the end result would be the same. Their countries would end up behaving as though they were similar to the republics that pledged their allegiance to Russia in the era of the Soviet Union.

"There, President Xi, I have had my say," He said in conclusion. "We have developed the means to make the countries of the European Union as receptive or submissive to the will of the Chinese government as we would wish them to be. The degree to which we want them to kowtow to our every whim is within our control."

"You have spoken well and comprehensively," Xi said to He. "Are there any others here in the room with us today who might wish to contribute an alternative perspective?"

Chapter Twenty

Not surprisingly, the first to speak up was the Editor-in-Chief of the state's daily rag tabloid, *The Global Times*. His name was Hu Xijin.

"Mr. President," said Hu, glancing at his notes, "There is a great deal to be taken into consideration when approaching what methods we may wish to use in infiltrating and destabilizing the countries that make up the European Union. The first thing to consider is their history. Their unity and camaraderie are not inconsiderable.

"Of the twenty-seven nations which make up the European Union, fifteen of them, sooner or later, were members of the Allied Forces which took on the Axis Powers. And the crux of those Axis Powers was Germany and Italy, two of the most powerful countries in the EU. They may have been on opposite sides, but these two alliances formed longstanding bonds whose remnants persist even to this day.

"Trying to pick these countries off one by one may be a difficult task. What we need to strive for is a common theme that will sever these old allegiances and cultivate a unifying ideology to which all of them yield and which all of them share. We must convince the man on the street and, ultimately, their heads of state by election or revolt, that the goals and objectives for creating a more cohesive European Union will best be served by adopting the socialist or Communist doctrines which we so fervently espouse."

"But just how do you propose that we bring about such a transformation?" interrupted Tuo Zhen, the Chief Editor and President of *The People's Daily*, the parent company of *The Global Times*.

"Look, Xijin," said Tuo, addressing his subordinate by his given name rather than his surname, "Between the two of us, our staffs represent the cream of the crop of propaganda journalists in the country. These guys don't write diplomatic tracts for the bureaucrats. They write grist for the common man to chew on. We want to whip them up into a frenzy. And we want them to demand that their leadership be responsive.

"There are only two things that concern every head of state; money and power. Few of their countries can support themselves financially based upon their nation's economy. Although the United States does not support the European Union in concept, they do support many of its members financially to ensure their economic viability as well as their obedience to the whims of the Allen Administration. As for the head of state's power, that derives from the people. Without that, they would change leaders. And to the current leaders, that would be a fate worse than death.

"As I have been observing the evolution of social norms which are conducive to the ideology of socialism in a number of nations in the EU, I have also been searching for potential leaders in those countries who would be inclined to implement regimes receptive to them. Some of those nations actually have registered Communist parties. But I'm sure all of them have Communist sympathizers.

"The five which have recognized Communist parties are France, Spain, Portugal, Ireland, and Germany. But Germany is a special case. I'll deal with that in a moment. Each of these parties has a senior member who may be inclined to seek a prominent position in their government if they believed that they could get their agenda implemented.

"The National Secretary of the French Communist Party is Fabien Roussel, a 54-year-old, lifelong Leftist who leads the 138,000-member group. Although he would have a hard time deposing the Right-Wing Marine Le Pen unless he collaborated with France's larger Socialist Party, he is quite charismatic and of an age where he would be of use to us for a good number of years. His Left-Wing competition would come from Olivier Faure, the First Secretary of the French Socialist Party who is 55 years old. However, Faure only ascended to his position within his own party when his opponent quit the party, taking a substantial part of the socialists' youth wing with him.

"The General Secretary of the Communist Party of

Spain is 59-year old Enrique Santiago. The mission statement of the PCE is to 'democratically participate in a revolutionary transformation of society and its political structures, overcoming the capitalist system and constructing socialism in the Spanish State, as a contribution to the transition to socialism worldwide, with our goals set in the realization of the emancipating ideal of Communism.' He would seem to be the right man with the right agenda at the right time.

"Jerónimo de Sousa is the Secretary-General of the Portuguese Communist Party. Their stated goal is to maintain its 'vanguard role in the service of the class interests of the workers.' Although he is 76 years old, he has held his position since 2005.

"As for Ireland, and by that I mean the Republic of Ireland but not Northern Ireland, their Communist party is led by Chairman John McCartan. They have rarely run candidates in national elections. They do, however, publish two newspapers, the weekly, *Unity*, and the monthly, *Socialist Voice*. Ireland will be a hard sell, but we owe them the courtesy to make the effort.

"Lastly comes Germany. As most of us in this room will remember, following World War II Germany was divided into four sectors under the control of the United States, the United Kingdom, France, and the Soviet Union. The first three were merged into the Federal Republic of

Germany and the fourth became the German Democratic Republic (GDR). The GDR became, by definition, Communist. This status continued until 1989, the fortieth anniversary of our own Communist revolution. It was in 1987 that U.S. President Reagan gave his 'Mr. Gorbachev, tear down this wall' speech. Two years later the German citizens did just that. The hostage Germans in the GDR seeking democracy fled to the West while those who were content or thriving under Communism either remained in place or were welcomed into one of the Eastern Bloc countries.

"Nonetheless, since 1969 there has been an officially recognized German Communist Party. Its leader is Patrik Köbele. It has a small but enthusiastic following. It will be a point from which we can start in reconstituting Communist ideology within Germany.

"As for the remainder of the countries in the European Union, many are, either in practice or reality, already socialist."

"Mr. Hu, I am quite impressed by the comprehensiveness of your research and report," said President Xi. "Therefore, I am going to appoint you as the point person for the introduction of new and subliminally undermining posts on social media against the capitalist regimes in the European Union. I sincerely hope that you prove worthy of my trust."

"I will do my very best," said Hu.

"Gentlemen, we are engaged in a war," concluded Xi. "It is not a war which will be won with guns or bombs. Indeed, I have no desire to destroy any of the substantive infrastructure of the European Union. Moreover, there is little doubt that the United States would come to the aid of their fellow NATO members as well as their other allies.

"Any engagement involving the United States has the potential of escalating into a nuclear holocaust. Although, as we saw in 2021 when we invaded Taiwan, it need not come to that. The American response was waged solely with conventional weapons. However, the risk still existed, and they had the weaponry on their aircraft carrier and in their submarines to cause inestimable damage.

"No, I want to take control of the European Union by stealth, not force. And if we're as good at capitalizing on the effects of propaganda as I believe us to be, the citizenry will sincerely believe that the changes in their political environment simply evolved over time as a natural result of the superiority of the socialist ideology over that of capitalism.

"I want each of you in this room to exercise your respective talents to their limits and render the bulk of the European continent a puppet regime of people of China."

Chapter Twenty-one

Following President Allen's August 2021 withdrawal of American troops from Afghanistan after a $2.3 trillion war, a fatally flawed operation of evacuating America's embassy personnel and civilians, and the failure to relocate a significant number of the Afghanis who had assisted the U.S military for 20 years, his popularity in his own country had plummeted to a near-historic low. There had been a corresponding drop in his prestige in foreign capitals. Hence, there was a vacuum throughout the Western World in search of heads of state worthy of widespread "trust and confidence".

Later in 2021 and throughout 2022 there had been clear signs of instability in the political *status quo* within the European Union. Perhaps it was a result of the work of China's Unit 61398 in Shanghai, the perpetual Left and Right oscillations of the ideological pendulum, or a bit of both. In any event, it would ultimately provide the Chinese with just the interval of vulnerability they needed to implement their agenda.

The six countries with registered Communist parties would be conducting elections for their heads of state in the coming four years. The first would be Italy in June of 2023. The second would be Portugal in October of the same year and Spain to close out the year in December. The fourth would be Ireland in September of 2025, with the fifth in Germany in September of 2025, and the last in France in April of 2027. This would give the Chinese ample time to achieve their ends of seizing both the political and ideological control of the European Union.

In March of 2018, Italy had held its last general election. The party with the greatest number of votes was named the Five Star Movement, but they did not garner a majority. After three months of negotiations, and because of their shared ideologies, they collaborated with the Center-Right Coalition and selected Giuseppe Conte as Prime Minister on the 1st of June. Subsequently, one of the constituencies withdrew their support for Conte and he resigned on August 20th, 2019. But a new coalition was formed with the Center-Left Democratic Party and Conte was sworn in for a second time as Prime Minister on September 5th, 2019.

Ever since the Chinese had begun their campaign of undermining conservative elected officials in Italy, the coalition of like-minded politicians had started to deteriorate. At the same time, the fortunes of the leader of the Democratic Party, the ultimate successor to the now-dissolved Italian Communist Party, Enrico Letta, had been in ascension as the posts by China to social media praised his ideas and ideology.

As Letta had previously met with former Prime

Minister Conte and shared his ideas with both Conte and the press as to what paths, social, political, & economic, Italy should take to best serve the interests of the Italian people, he had become quite a known quantity to the man on the street. He was a married man whose wife was a journalist and he had three sons. He projected an image of stability for which the Italian people longed. In the general election in June of 2023, Letta narrowly defeated his opponent, Mario Draghi, who had been in office for just over two years following the resignation of Conte in 2021.

The next election within the European Union among countries with Communist parties would take place in Portugal in October. Six months out from the election, the Socialist Party held 39% of the vote versus the Social Democrat's 26%. The head of the Portuguese Communist Party was Jerónimo de Sousa. The PCP organizes in its ranks industrial and office workers, small and medium farmers, intellectuals and technical workers, small and medium shopkeepers, and industrialists who fight for democracy and socialism. The party considers itself the legitimate pursuer of the Portuguese people's best traditions of struggle and their progressive and revolutionary achievements throughout their history.

Every year, during the first weekend of September, the party holds a festival called the Avante! Festival. After taking place in different locations around Lisbon, like the Lisbon International Fair, Ajuda, or Loures, it was being held in Amora. The party considered this campaign to be the only way to avoid the boycott organized by the owners of the previous festival grounds, a boycott that ultimately resulted in the Festival not being held in 1987. The festival attracts hundreds of thousands of visitors. The events themselves consist of a three-day festival of music, with hundreds of Portuguese and international bands and artists across five different stages, ethnography, gastronomy, debates, a books and music fair, theater, cinema, and sporting events. Several foreign Communist parties also participate.

Because of the composition of the Portuguese population and their political leanings, the outcome of the election in Portugal legitimately and straightforwardly came out in favor of Jerónimo de Sousa, the Secretary-General of the Portuguese Communist Party and standard-bearer for the socialists. That gave them two out of six. The next election would be held in Spain in December.

The Spanish legislature consists of two houses, the Senate and the Congress of Deputies. The Senate has 208 seats and they are filled by the electorate voting for a candidate by name. The Congress has 348 seats which are voted on by party. In the previous election which took place on November 20th, 2019, the largest vote winner was either a member of the Spanish Socialist Workers Party (PSOE) in the Congress or the PSOE itself.

The winner of the election in the Senate was the leader of the PSOE, Pedro Sánchez, whose party controls 110 seats. In the Congress, his party won the most seats, 108. He has served as the Prime Minister of Spain since that time.

The PSOE is the successor to *Izquierada Unida*, or United Left, which was created in 1986 as a collaboration of seven smaller liberal and progressive parties. Of those seven parties, the Communist Party of Spain led by Enrique Santiago is the only one that remains in existence. But the PSOE is the entity that constitutes the permanent federation of parties.

Communists, socialists, or Left-Wingers had won three straight European Union federal elections. The work of the Chinese propagandists in social media had most assuredly had an influence in at least two of those elections. And their work was not yet done. They would do their best to orchestrate the outcome of the upcoming elections in Ireland, Germany, and France over the next four years. But President Xi Jinping and the Communist Party of China had no intention of waiting four years to move ahead with their agenda.

Back in Washington, President Allen had been closely following the election results in Italy, Spain, and Portugal. But not with the concern with which his predecessor would have. He believed that he could cordially negotiate with like-minded liberals the world over. After all, notwithstanding China's world-domination agenda, he thought that he and Xi Jinping could have an amicable and mutually productive relationship.

The most recent development had been China's overture to Afghanistan following the American withdrawal of military forces. On August 16th, 2021, China's English tabloid, *The Global Times*, spoke of China's border with Afghanistan. While nominal, its location made it crucial geopolitically. *The Bloomberg New Energy Finance Limited* reported that Afghanistan had large deposits of gold, iron, copper, zinc, lithium, and other rare earth metals valued at over $1 trillion. It said "Afghanistan may hold . . . millions [of] tons of rare earth elements . . ." Rare earth elements are used for making key components of cell phones, cameras, computer disks, TVs, and other equipment. They also have applications in the clean energy and defense industries.

Afghanistan had vast reserves of lithium, a key component in building the lithium-ion batteries that powered everything from mobile phones to electric vehicles to new generations of submarines. China led the world's lithium-ion battery supply chain market. Its getting control of untapped deposits of lithium in Afghanistan would prove an advantage for Beijing in its evolving competition with the U.S. and Europe for resources. In 2019, the U.S. had imported 80% of its rare earth minerals from China, while the EU got 98% of these materials from the same source.

Chapter Twenty-two

Throughout 2023, the political, economic, and military leadership in the People's Republic of China had been keeping a close eye on the recent developments in the European Union. A significant number of the heads of state were socialists, Left-Leaning, or subject to the whims of the electorate which the authors of the slanted social media posts had become adept at manipulating. Their economies had either knowingly or unwittingly become dependent upon China's manufacturers and retailers for their day-to-day consumer goods. And the network of 5G webcams had maintained a watchful observance on any new developments in weaponry so as to be prepared with a superior response. It was time to take the initiative to wrest the EU out from under the onerous influence and virtual control of both NATO and the United States.

Presidents Jinping and Russia's Vladimir Putin had exhibited an outwardly cordial relationship for a long time. After all, their countries' underlying ideologies were essentially the same. However, the manner in which they were administered and enforced varied in both degree and method.

For a number of years, the Russian Navy and the People's Liberation Army Navy had conducted joint naval exercises in the South China Sea. In recent years they had moved on to "blue water" exercises in the Western Pacific. Although all of these exercises had been meant as a show of both mutual respect and camaraderie, neither of the two men was under any illusion that, should the occasion and need arise, they would gladly fire upon one another in defense of their respective homelands.

The Russian Navy had easy access to both the Atlantic and Pacific Oceans. Their Eastern border included a stretch on the Pacific, but access to the Atlantic was a little more tricky. They had to pass the Scandinavian peninsula and then make their way through what was referred to as the GIUK (Greenland – Iceland – United Kingdom) Gap. Notwithstanding the availability of the closely monitored English Channel, the gap was composed of two additional routes which included the waters between Ireland and Iceland, and those between Iceland and Greenland. There was, of course, the Irish Sea, but sailing between the English island and the island of Ireland was not only a tedious business but would take them perilously close to the headquarters of the UK's submarine service at Her Majesty's Naval Base Clyde at Faslane on what is called Gare Loch in Scotland.

The Chinese Navy had long wanted an expedient and secure passage from their East Coast to the Atlantic Ocean, but until now that was essentially limited to the One Road route by way of the South China Sea, the Strait of Malacca, the Indian Ocean, the Suez Canal, the Mediterranean Sea, and the Strait of Gibraltar. The commercial container carriers also sought a similar route for financial reasons. The easiest solution was the Northern Sea Route, also referred to as the Polar Silk Road, along the Arctic coast of Russia, past the Scandinavian peninsula, and through the English Channel. But the European port fees were exorbitant.

Now they had an in which had eluded them five years earlier when they had tried to establish a foothold on the West Coast of Greenland. Then, China had approached the government of the Kingdom of Denmark which exercised sovereignty over the autonomous constituent state of Greenland and sought their permission to build ports on its West Coast. But intervention by President Jefferson on behalf of the United States and NATO was meant to prevent China from getting Denmark's approval. However, Greenland had used the terms of the Home Rule Act of 1979 which granted it the right to establish its own legislature distinct from the Danish Parliament to overrule the government in Copenhagen. Only a sea battle between the United States and China off the West Coast of Greenland in 2020 had brought that incident of adventurism to an end.

But it was now 2023, and President Jefferson had been succeeded by President Allen who saw Xi Jinping as a sometimes ally in the battle for political causes and China as a potential partner in such ventures. Moreover, Denmark was a member of the European Union whose balance of trade with China had dipped deeply into the red. If China was allowed to reinvest some of that money from Denmark in the Danish kingdom, both in the port of Aarhus and on the island of Greenland, they could kill two birds with one stone.

The port of Aarhus is the largest container port in Denmark and, with its outstanding efficiency, the port is one of the most productive in Denmark or, for that matter, Europe. In addition, the port has the capacity to handle the largest container ships in the world. Finally, the distance, and thus the expense, of sailing to Aarhus via the Polar Silk Road was only two-thirds that of the One Road route. China would make state-subsidized capital loans to Denmark to enlarge the port by adding more container ship docks while building a Chinese port for warships on Greenland's East Coast. President Allen would turn a blind eye to the Chinese investment in Denmark while Greenland would receive hefty amounts of Chinese yuan to pay the workers trucked in from the West Coast cities to build the East Coast naval port.

That naval base on Greenland's East Coast would give Chinese surface vessels and submarines an unfettered straight shot through one of the paths of the GIUK Gap while remaining in Danish territorial waters. It would also provide the ability to maintain close observance of NATO ship movements. The financial straits in which China had placed the nations of the European Union would eventually yield further, if not as dramatic, benefits.

In order to negotiate the concessions which China
desired from Denmark, ministers of foreign affairs, trade,
and the military would be dispatched to Copenhagen to meet
with their opposite numbers from Denmark. The Minister of
Foreign Affairs was Wang Yi who had assumed his position
in 2013 and was fluent in English. The Minister for
Commerce was Wang Wentao. A man who had once sold
photocopiers, Wang was appointed minister in 2020.
Representing the military would be the Minister of National
Defense, General Wei Fenghe. Appointed in 2018, Wei had
been in the People's Liberation Army Air Force (PLAAF)
since the age of 16 and had risen to the rank of Commander
of the PLA Rocket Force. The three would fly to
Copenhagen during the second week of January 2024 aboard
one of the PLAAF's two tri-jet Tupolev Tu-154 airliners
used for ferrying dignitaries and parked at Beijing's Daxing
International Airport. The 4,500-mile flight would take well
over eight and one-half hours.

They would be meeting with Denmark's Minister of
Foreign Affairs, Jeppe Kofod, Minister for Industry,
Business, and Financial Affairs, Simon Kollerup, and
Minister of Defense, Trine Bramsen. Kofod was appointed
in 2019 and, like his Chinese counterpart, also spoke fluent
English as a result of his years at Harvard earning his Master
of Public Administration (MPA) degree. Kollerup had also
been appointed in 2019. Bramsen, one of the few female
defense ministers in the world, was, like her two colleagues,

appointed to her office in 2019.

The Chinese aircraft arrived in Denmark's airspace in the wee hours of the morning on Tuesday, January 9th. Customarily emissaries of such high rank were met by diplomats of equivalent rank from their host country. But these meetings were, if not classified, at a minimum very low-key. After they were "wheels down" at Copenhagen's Kastrup Airport, the Tupolev jet taxied to a hangar a long distance from the main terminal.

There its passengers disembarked with no fanfare whatsoever, climbed into a single black town car, and departed the airfield. Rather than going to one of the city's three Five Star hotels, they were driven to the modest Chinese Embassy in Hellerup, four and one-quarter miles North of Copenhagen's city center. They were each shown to their room where they promptly went to bed. The next three days of meetings were expected to be tedious and exhausting.

All of the meetings were to take place out of sight of the citizens of Denmark inside the embassy. One-on-one meetings, with or without a translator present, would take place in one of the few administrative offices. Meetings of all six government officials would take place in the conference room/dining room. The meetings would commence at 10:00AM on Tuesday and continue until whatever time was dictated by their progress on Thursday.

Chapter Twenty-three

On Tuesday morning, the three Danish ministers were each picked up at their homes by their personal drivers in their staff cars. On their way to the Chinese Embassy in Hellerup, Ministers Kofod, Kollerup, and Bramsen all stopped by their respective offices to pick up folios containing the most recent briefing papers which they could glance at before they arrived and to which they could refer throughout their three days of negotiations. Much to his chagrin, for three days the two Foreign Ministers would be meeting in the Ambassador's office. The upside would be that he could remain in his residence on the upper floor.

Conveniently, because Foreign Minister Wang Yi spoke English and his partner for the meetings, Foreign Minister Kofod, also spoke English, it being taught from elementary school in every school district in Denmark, they had no need for a translator in the room. However, one was always available should some nuance in the languages need clarification. Theirs would be the most crucial and intense of the negotiations.

Even though the meetings of the two ministers of trade and the two ministers of defense would require translators, they would meet in smaller side offices to that of the ambassador. Once the fundamentals of the proposals which each Chinese minister would be setting forth were on the table and their partner's initial reactions registered and responded to, the first of the six-person (eight if one included the two translators) meetings would convene in the dining room. It was there that the intricacies of a multidisciplinary agreement would be worked out.

Of all of the preliminary meetings, the one between the two Foreign Ministers would the most protracted. Their success, of course, would be predicated upon the parallels between the politics and diplomatic goals of the People's Republic of China and the Kingdom of Denmark. The outcome of the federal elections conducted in Denmark in 2019 boded well from the point of view of the Chinese.

The winner of the election was what was then referred to as the "Red Bloc" which was comprised of parties supporting the leader of the Social Democrats, Mette Frederiksen, the Social Liberals, the Socialist People's Party, and the Red – Green (or, colloquially, the "Traffic Light") Alliance. On June 6th the incumbent Prime Minister, Lars Løkke Rasmussen, from the Center-Right liberal party had tendered his resignation. It was then up to Frederiksen to form a new coalition government. On June 27th she was appointed Prime Minister.

The general elections of June 2023 reflected the same attitudes and preferences of the electorate as had those of 2019. Mette Frederiksen and her majority in the legislature prevailed and they would hold office for the next four years barring any unanticipated developments. That put Ministers

Wang and Kofod on the same side of the ideological fence.

The two Foreign Ministers had first met at the meeting of the United Nations General Assembly in 2020. Their introductions took place at a reception in the Chinese Consulate at 520 12th Avenue in New York City on the Hudson River at the opposite end of 41st Street from the United Nations building on the East River.

As they both spoke English, their casual exchanges were not diminished by the stilted linguistic twists of an interpreter. They had struck it off well and both had remarked as to some of the similarities in their respective governments' policies. Clearly, the approaches and application of their ideologies were distinctly different, but the purported goals were not so dissimilar. The universality of the ends of their two educational systems, for example, was one of the tenets of their cultures upon which they could both agree.

While the discussion between the two Foreign Ministers was both conceptual and philosophical, that between the two economic ministers was frank, if not blunt. As the minister from the guest country, Minister Wang Wentao let Minister Kollerup, the minister from the host country, go first. Kollerup simply made some generic opening remarks and then turned the floor over to Wang.

"Minister Kollerup," began Wang, "Yours is a

prosperous country. But no country can be *too* prosperous. There are three key points which I would like to make in opening. The first is that the only truly domestic economy which is functioning profitably in Denmark is that of the "mom & pop" brick and mortar retail stores. They are autonomous. China has no impact upon them whatsoever.

"The second point is that the chain stores, be they department stores, electronics stores, hardware stores, . . . whatever, have been bought up by dummy Chinese corporations registered in Denmark and which are owned by venture capitalists back in China. The Danes benefit from the low prices but the profits accrue to the Chinese.

"Finally, virtually all online purchases profit China. Some people simply go to AliExpress and the like knowing full well that they are buying from Chinese vendors. The others go to what appear to be sites in Denmark. But those sites' corporate headquarters are nothing but dummy corporations opened by the Chinese and registered in Denmark." Kollerup could remain silent no longer.

"That cannot be!" exclaimed the minister. "My country maintains meticulous business records. Those corporations all have native Danes as their CEOs and boards of directors made up of my countrymen."

"In that, you are absolutely correct," said Wang. "And they are being handsomely compensated for their 'management' of those corporations. But make no mistake about it. They are taking their orders from Beijing. Now I think it time that we get to the 'real' purpose for my visit to your lovely country.

"Hundreds of years ago, the Silk Road was made famous by Marco Polo. He brought spices, pasta, and, of course, silk back from Asia to Europe. That route is now referred to in China as the One Belt. Added to that was the One Road. It is the sea route that passes through the South China Sea, the Strait of Malacca, the Indian Ocean, the Suez Canal, the Mediterranean Sea, and the Strait of Gibraltar. Together they form the Belt and Road Initiative (BRI).

"But a new route now exists. Because of the receding Arctic ice cap, the route from the Pacific to the Atlantic along Russia's Northern coastline has become navigable year-round. And it is one-third shorter than the One Road. China needs ports capable of handling container ships at the Western end of the Polar Silk Road. That, my friend, is where Denmark comes in.

"Aarhus is the largest container port in Europe. Due to its efficiency, it is also purportedly the most productive. And it has the capacity to handle the largest container ships in the world, many of which are owned or leased by Chinese companies. And, as I said previously, the distance, and thus the expense, of sailing to Aarhus via the Polar Silk Road is only two-thirds that of the One Road route.

"I am authorized to extend to you an offer of a low-interest loan, subsidized by my country, to expand the port facilities at Aarhus, the new docks to be reserved for the exclusive use of Chinese ships. In exchange, we will, of course, pay all applicable port fees and taxes. This will allow China to get its goods to European markets more quickly and more cheaply. And it will generate tremendous revenues for Denmark."

"But that would compromise Denmark's autonomy!" protested Kollerup.

"It would do no such thing," responded Wang. "China has no desire to interfere in the day-to-day functioning of the Danish government. This is a business deal; nothing more. Why don't you take the time to think this over while the four other ministers are meeting? There will also be a second proposal which will be placed upon the table. When the six of us sit down together, I think they will see the wisdom in pursuing this venture."

Minister Kollerup had been taken totally by surprise. The forwardness and the arrogance of Minister Wang had put him off. But his logic was unassailable. Expanding Aarhus would be both prestigious in the commercial marine community and the revenues handsome. While they waited for the joint meeting to commence, he gave the proposal due consideration.

Chapter Twenty-four

Perhaps the most interesting and intense discussion between two ministers that Tuesday morning was taking place between Minister of National Defense, General Wei Fenghe, of the People's Republic of China and Danish Minister of Defense Trine Bramsen.

After Minister Bramsen made a few brief introductory remarks, General Wei provided her with a succinct synopsis of the proposal which Minister Wang had presented to Minister Kollerup. Bramsen did not realize it at that point, but this was to be the proverbial "carrot". Then Wei hit her with the "stick".

In 2021, over the objections of Republican President John Jefferson of the United States and in accordance with the vote of Greenland's parliament, the Chinese government had been contracted to rebuild or expand three airports and accompanying nearby port facilities on the West Coast of Greenland. These ports were ostensibly to be for the docking of Chinese container ships. But these container ships were accompanied by vessels from the People's Liberation Army Navy as "escorts". When the warships appeared to take on the expanded ports on Greenland's West Coast as their home ports, the United States Navy intervened to take the vessels out.

Now, Minister Wei was proposing that China be allowed to construct a naval base on Greenland's East Coast overlooking one of the passages of the GIUK Gap. Minister Bramsen was, as was Minister Kollerup, taken totally by surprise. But the stakes were even higher than had they been in 2021.

The expansion of the port of Aarhus would be worth millions upon millions of kroner to the economy of Denmark. And the building of the naval base on Greenland's East Coast would provide hundreds of jobs to Greenlanders living on the island's West Coast for whom the only two industries currently were catching fish & harvesting shellfish and tourism. It would serve as a win – win for Denmark; added revenue for the government on the European continent and the need for fewer subsidies for the outposts on Greenland.

Minister Bramsen would have to give this proposal serious thought. And while she was thinking, she periodically asked General Wei a question or prevailed upon him to further clarify some point in his proposal. All the while the two other pairs of ministers were engaged in further discussions of their own.

Shortly before noon, word went out from each of the three pairs that they had concluded their preliminary talks and were ready to meet *en masse*. They convened in the dining room. Moments later, food and drinks were deposited in front of each of the six ministers. The translators were expected to eat in the background.

As the senior Danish minister, Foreign Minister Kofod stood, raised his glass of Tyrrell's Vat 1 Semillon white wine, and offered a toast to the ultimate success of the three days of negotiations. His five peers stood and raised their glasses. The food would undoubtedly be excellent and the Semillon would serve as an effective lubricant for the remainder of the day. He then commenced his perfunctory summary of the events of the day so far.

"Today is the first of three days of what I have been led to believe will be both productive and beneficial negotiations for the People's Republic of China and the Kingdom of Denmark. This morning Foreign Minister Wang and I began our discussions with some preliminary statements regarding the current state of diplomatic relations between our respective countries. We came to some general agreement on the state of affairs in our two nations and what each country could do to enhance the political, economic, and military status and stability of the others.

"There was little disagreement as to the general outline of the proposals which Minister Wang put on the table with regard to the continued cordial diplomatic relations between China and Denmark. Where things became a little dicier was when we got into specifics. There were no insurmountable obstacles, but I would be being less than candid if I didn't admit that the devil, or devils, as they say, are in the details. Those details entailed your talks.

"This morning Ministers Wang Wentao and Simon Kollerup discussed the economic state of affairs of Denmark. They then moved on to a specific proposal from Minister Wang with respect to the port of Aarhus. As you may know, Aarhus is the largest and most efficient container port in Europe. It can also handle the world's largest container ships.

"China has adopted a new facet to its established Belt and Road Initiative, or BRI. Because the polar ice cap is receding, it has made the Northern Sea Route navigable nearly year-round. The Chinese refer to this path as the Polar Silk Road in honor of the original Silk Road once used to carry goods from the Orient to Europe. They are in need of a port at the Western end of the Polar Silk Road terminating in the European Union. Aarhus fills that bill.

"Minister Wang's plan calls for the expansion of Aarhus by adding piers which will be for the exclusive use of Chinese ships. The construction of the piers will be paid for using low-interest state-subsidized loans from China. The additional docking fees and the taxes collected on the goods imported will not only cover the cost of building the piers but will, more importantly, supplement the state coffers. As a result, both China and Denmark will benefit from the project.

"While Simon Kollerup and Wang Wentao were discussing finances and trade, Ministers Bramsen and Wei Fenghe were speaking of military matters. Several years ago, China built or refurbished three airfields and their accompanying ports on Greenland's West Coast. This was ostensibly to allow it to use Western Greenland as a transshipment point for Chinese consumer goods bound for Western Europe and the Americas.

"When the United States became aware of the activity, it had approached Denmark's government to prevent China's agenda based upon its concerns relative to national security. But Greenland had enough autonomy to allow it to proceed. China used the improved ports as home bases for a number of their military 'escort' ships. The United States lost no time in issuing a threat that they would not tolerate concentrations of Chinese military vessels so close to America's East Coast. When China did not retreat, the U.S. Navy proceeded to eliminate the potential naval threat by force.

"But now, China is proposing to construct a naval base on Greenland's *East* Coast. Such a naval base would have multiple benefits, all accruing to China. First, it would give China a presence in the Atlantic. Second, it would provide an ideal vantage point from which to monitor enemy naval activity in the GIUK Gap. And, finally, it is a nearly perfect location from which to launch an attack on any

Western government's naval activity by which it felt threatened or which portended a new naval strategy.

"One might ask what the benefits are which would accrue to Denmark by the construction of a major naval installation on Greenland's East Coast. First, let me state that the government of Denmark in no way fears or feels threatened by the proximity of Chinese naval forces. That having been said, the construction of a theater naval base is a tremendous undertaking.

"As I stated previously, Greenland's two main sources of revenue are the reaping of the wealth of marine resources by which it is surrounded and, secondarily, tourism. But the two combined cannot provide employment opportunities for the entire working-age population of the island. For the next several years, the construction of the naval facilities would provide work for a significant number of workers from both Greenland's East and West Coasts. The base would require not only docking and maintenance facilities but, in the long run, housing, food services, and the customary retail outlets necessary to support the large number of sailors, soldiers, and civilians permanently residing there.

"Before these meetings break up on Thursday, it is my sincerest wish that we may come to an agreement whereby the diplomatic, economic, and military needs of our two nations may be both satisfied and enhanced. To that end, I ask that each of you devote your efforts to that outcome."

Chapter Twenty-five

Not surprisingly, the remainder of Tuesday's discussions focused on the reactions to Denmark's potential decisions by the members of the European Union, the nations that constitute NATO, and the United States. The first to arrive would be the political fallout from capitals across Europe regarding Denmark's apparent alliance with the People's Republic of China and its implications for the remaining countries in the European Union. Then would be speculation as to the creation of a Chinese port on the European continent, followed by the repulsion of creating a Chinese military installation in Western Europe. Finally, after consultation with his Secretary of State, Secretary of Commerce, and his National Security Council, President Robert Allen would weigh in.

The trend in the most recent federal elections in the European Union, as well as the orientation of those heads of state already in office, was toward not only liberalism but socialism, the most notable exception being Marine Le Pen in France. Consequently, even though Le Pen was not shy about exerting her influence as the EU's strongman, she was simply outnumbered by her adversaries. In the end, it was concluded that the Kingdom of Denmark's economic and arm's length military alliance with the People's Republic of China would have no lasting ill effects.

Just over two years earlier, on Friday, October 22nd, 2021, French Armed Forces Minister Florence Parly had told a NATO defense ministers conference that they should not fear the European Union's defense plans and claimed that the United States would benefit from any strengthened European capacities. These comments had been made to respond to months of uncertainty about the EU's latest efforts to develop weapons and forces and as to whether they would be perceived as in competition with the NATO alliance.

"When I hear some defensive statements on European defense and when I observe certain threats, including within this organization, I say: 'don't be afraid!',", she told a session that included the EU's top diplomat, Josep Borrell Fontelles. "European defense isn't being built in opposition to NATO, quite the contrary: a stronger Europe will contribute to a strengthened and more resilient alliance."

Then American Secretary of Defense Lloyd Austin reacted positively, saying he would welcome a robust European defense, repeating the sentiments of a joint statement issued in September by French President La Pen and U.S. President Allen. "What we'd like to see are initiatives that are complementary to the types of things that NATO is doing," Austin told a news conference. He reinforced his spurring on of NATO allies to live up to their "number one job" of "credible deterrence and defense".

The Secretary of Defense also pointed out that there was no conflict between the European and American agendas with respect to the Indo-Pacific theater, saying that NATO members were working together to respond to the ever-growing threat from the burgeoning Chinese military machine. The previous month, Washington had signed a pact with Great Britain and Australia to supply the Australian Navy with $90 billion worth of nuclear submarines. The loss of that contract, which had tentatively gone to France, had cost the French government that $90 billion. The fallout from the transaction had caused significant friction among the French, British, and Americans.

At the meeting, Austin pledged to "collectively work to ensure that the Indo-Pacific . . . region remained free and open." He reiterated that the United States would continue its efforts to prepare Taiwan to defend itself from any threat by the Chinese Communists. But the one thing that had never been stated explicitly by any member of the Allen Administration was whether the United States would come to the direct military support of Taiwan if it were to be invaded by China again as the Jefferson Administration had done in January of 2021.

Britain, no longer a member of the European Union, had said that the EU had a supporting role to play in NATO. However, Britain's Defense Secretary Ben Wallace had characterized any attempt to build an EU army as a distraction, derogatorily pointing out that it would be a "red herring" and that there was "absolutely no point in sticking European berets on a whole load of people". As it stood, of the 27 EU states 21 of them were also members of the 30-member NATO alliance.

What was notable was that the Eastern European states in the European Union remained intimidated by Russia and feared the exhibiting of any shift away from NATO. The NATO Secretary-General himself, Jens Stoltenberg, had warned against duplication. "What is needed are more capabilities, not new structures," he'd told a news conference.

* * *

The discussion among the six high-level bureaucrats from China and Denmark continued throughout the remainder of the afternoon. The subjects focused upon the conceptual and the ramifications of the actions they were contemplating. As the day wore on, what became increasingly apparent was that the entire undertaking would require the two nations to conduct a delicate geopolitical balancing act. What also became more and more clear was that while the Danes were inclined to practice international diplomacy with a velvet glove, the Chinese tended to prefer to impose their will with an iron fist.

At the end of the business day, the three members of

the Danish delegation were each picked up at the Chinese Embassy by their respective drivers and driven home. The three Chinese representatives dined with the ambassador and then retired to three private bedrooms which they had commandeered from three members of the embassy staff. Those staff members had been forced to double up with other of their colleagues.

Tuesday's discussions were centered upon the diplomatic, economic, and military details of the plan. Fortunately, the diplomatic negotiators and military strategists back in Beijing were masters of their crafts and quite detail-oriented. They had thought of all the questions the Danes might ask and prepared succinct answers. During the day the fine points were negotiated and agreed upon. Tuesday's lunches were taken in the meeting rooms where each pair of representatives could continue their discussions unimpeded.

The meeting conducted on Thursday, January 11th, was a joint session of all six delegates in the dining room and was employed to iron out last-minute details. Finally, there was the task of composing the formal announcement of the alliance which would be made to the European Council at their meeting in Brussels on the following Thursday, January 18th. The European Council's meetings are colloquially referred to as "European Union Summits".

The summit meetings are chaired by the President of

the European Council. The is an aggregate body of the heads of state of all the EU nations. It meets for the purpose of selecting and refining the political directions and priorities of the EU. The High Representative of the Union for Foreign Affairs and Security Policy is an ad hoc member of the Council and it was to him, Josep Borrell Fontelles of the Spanish Socialist Workers' Party, that much of the presentation that day would be addressed.

Having completed a First Draft of the announcement, the group took a break for a non-working lunch during which they discussed informal subjects such as families and personal interests. It also gave each of them time to decompress. The prospect of the following week's meeting had put them all somewhat on edge. When the work resumed, the six perseverated over each word as they knew full well that the statement would be dissected word by word in the coming week. Finally, the work was done and the three Danes took their leave of their Chinese counterparts.

It was after dark, but still not even 6:00PM, as the Chinese delegation reboarded their Tupolev Tu-154 aircraft for the return flight to Beijing. No sooner had the cabin door been closed at the airport than the bottles of the best Western spirits were broken out and each representative was poured a stiff drink of their favorite alcoholic beverage. They spoke at length as the effects of their drinks relieved three days of built-up tensions. They were not yet even one hour into their flight before they were all asleep.

Chapter Twenty-six

Throughout the first three years of President Robert Allen's tenure, his Democrat administration had not felt threatened by the Communist Party of China. Their capturing of the contract to build the European Union's 5G and internet networks had caused no concern in the Nation's Capital. But the city of Washington was now in the throws of its every four-year presidential campaign.

The conventional wisdom was that the Democrat convention would nominate President Allen for a second four-year term. But this year had brought a wild card. Clint Anderson, the hard-core conservative Republican governor of Texas, had emerged from obscurity to become the front runner in the race for the Republican nomination. He was an adamant and vocal Hawk who had seen China as the United States' preeminent threat in geopolitics and the military realm for well over two decades.

Russian President Putin's administration, along with his country's economy and military, had been in decline for those same two decades while China's Xi Jinping had, for all intents and purposes, had himself declared President for Life. He still had Taiwan in his sights, having already staged one unsuccessful invasion, while he was now threatening the security and political self-determination of both Japan and Australia. It had been their pledge to align themselves with Washington in any future military undertaking in support of Taiwan which had antagonized Xi. Unlike Allen, Anderson had been unequivocal in the expression of his backing of Taiwan.

Over the weekend of the13[th] and 14th of January, Denmark's Prime Minister Mette Frederiksen had spent a significant portion of her time on the telephone providing the other EU heads of state with a confidential heads up on the joint Chinese/Danish announcement which would be made on the 19th. She had also given a courtesy call to the United Kingdom's Prime Minister Boris Johnson as the UK was a former member of the EU and they still played an integral role in the economy of the European Union. It was that phone call which would pose a significant threat to the Chinese/Danish alliance.

During Johnson's nearly five years in office, he had had numerous occasions to cross paths with Texas Governor Anderson and they had hit it off. Moreover, they shared a similar dread of China's explicit expressed aim at global hegemony. As an afterthought, Johnson picked up the phone on Sunday evening after several glasses of Tignanello, a fine red wine, and called his friend and political ally Anderson.

Johnson thought it only right that he share with the governor his advance notice of the alliance that Denmark and China would be sharing with the European Union on Friday.

Anderson, ever the shrewd politician and tactician, saw this revelation as an opportunity to broaden his base of support both domestically and internationally. He placed a phone call to President Marine La Pen of France, the European Union's strongman and a fellow conservative and Hawk, and, after a few brief cordial exchanges, told her that Boris Johnson had spilled the beans as to the joint announcement to be released by Denmark on Friday morning.

Anderson asked La Pen if she would be kind enough to invite him to join her as her guest at the European Union summit and arrange for him to be allowed to speak at the opening of Friday's general session. As a gesture of goodwill to an up-and-coming American politician of a similar stripe, she agreed. After the President of the EU gaveled Friday's general session to order, Anderson would be permitted to make what was characterized to her as a brief opening statement.

The week flew by. On Monday and Tuesday, Clint Anderson conducted the business of state as was his custom. But on Tuesday evening he boarded a Lufthansa Airbus 330-300 flight at Bergstrom International Airport in Austin headed for the overnight journey to Frankfurt, Germany. There he had a four-hour layover until he caught a Lufthansa Airbus A320 Sharklet for the brief one-hour flight to Brussels. It was 3:00PM on Wednesday afternoon when he arrived at the Brussels Marriott Grand Hotel Place. He went to his room and, after a long hot shower, headed straight for bed to catch up on the sleep he lost on the flight from Austin.

He awoke in the middle of the night and called room service. He ordered a typical Texas-sized breakfast. It was at his hotel room door in twenty minutes and he let the steward bring it in and set it up before tipping him and letting him out. Afterward, he reclined on the couch and watched the international cable TV to see what developments were leading the news. Of course, there was the obligatory story about the upcoming EU summit.

After lounging around his room until late morning, Anderson decided he needed a change of scenery. He pulled open the blackout draperies and then the brocade drapes. He found that it was snowing hard on this mid-January day and the thermometer on the television screen told him that it was well below freezing. He had clearly not packed for this sort of weather.

He threw on some casual clothes and took the elevator down to the spacious and luxurious lobby. He walked through a portal to the atrium shopping center next door. First, he went to a shoe store where he purchased a pair of leather hiking boots with Vibram soles to negotiate the sidewalks and streets of Brussels. Then he went into a sporting goods store and purchased both a down parka, fully-equipped with a hood, and a pair of Polartec gloves. He took his new attire back to his room and put everything on. Only then did he deem himself prepared to take on a Belgian Winter storm.

He didn't plan to be out past lunchtime as he needed to leave himself that afternoon to write the speech he would be delivering to the General Assembly of the European Union on Friday morning. Nonetheless, the fresh, cold air and brisk walk helped to finish clearing his head from his nearly twenty-four hours of travel. When he returned to his room he would be ready to start writing. He would even have time to have his speech reviewed by a trusted advisor.

* * *

Clint Anderson was the son of a highly-respected Texas district court judge. His father had wanted him to go into the family business but Clint had developed other plans. After graduating from Regents School, a classical Christian prep school, Anderson had attended the United States Naval Academy courtesy of a Texas congressman and family friend's nomination. He'd majored in Engineering with a minor in Political Science.

After graduation, he'd been sent to San Diego. He put in his at-sea time on *Spruance* class destroyers. After his discharge, he returned to Texas and took up administrative work in the oil business while beginning to dabble in local politics. He started with Austin but soon moved on to Travis County. That led, in short order, to becoming a rising star in the Texas 10th Congressional District. Because of the redistricting in 2003, he found himself participating in the 25th Congressional District's activities.

Clint Anderson was approached on numerous occasions to run for the House of Representatives from the 25th District, but he begged off, focusing on his work in the oil business and resisting the seductive temptation to move into the world of Washington politics. One day he decided that, with an outgoing conservative Republican governor, it was time to run for the Governor's Mansion. His support was overwhelming and he seemed to simply glide into the statehouse.

But it was now 2024. The national political winds had blown both ways, conservative and liberal, over the past several administrations and elections. But the nation's population and political persuasion were currently drifting to the Right. And that was just the political weather forecast Anderson needed to wade into national political waters.

Now was his moment. China was making its move. The prevailing sentiments around the world were running against them. But no one was standing up to oppose them. Anderson saw his opportunity. And the General Assembly of the European Union was the venue where he could make an indelible impression upon the players on the world stage.

Chapter Twenty-seven

The cabinet of President Robert Allen, as well as those members of his inner circle of advisors, appeared to have been assembled as though someone had gone down a list of liberal interest groups and simply checked off the boxes next to them until all the boxes had been checked. There was but one secretary who did not fit that mold; Secretary of State Charles Wainwright, a holdover from the Jefferson Administration. The Secretary was a retired four-star admiral and former Chairman of the Joint Chiefs of Staff.

When Governor Anderson learned that he would be allowed to address the European Union, he had gotten in touch with his old friend, Secretary of State Wainwright. Wainwright had been the first cabinet member chosen for the previous Republican administration's cabinet by John Jefferson, having been selected on November 16, 2016. Anderson asked him if he would be willing to review his speech before he delivered it to make sure he had not made any misstatements or stepped into any minefields.

That afternoon Wainwright would be waiting by his personal FAX machine in his office at State for Anderson's DRAFT to arrive. Although the document came through government phone lines, he needn't worry about it showing up anywhere else as FAXes had been superseded by more technologically-advanced devices and his was the only FAX machine on the seventh floor in Foggy Bottom. Wainwright would return it to Anderson with any corrections or deletions and it would arrive in the Business Office on the ground floor of the Marriott which remained open 24 hours a day.

Early on Thursday afternoon, Anderson sat down at the desk in his suite with a pad of yellow legal-sized paper and a handful of pens and started to write. His agenda would be to preempt Denmark's announcement and make it very clear to the members of the EU just how his administration would react if the Chinese were to proceed as planned. His high poll numbers back in the States would give his warning significant impact.

Late in the afternoon, Anderson went to the Marriott's Business Center and sent his FAX to Secretary Wainwright in Washington. A couple of hours later, he heard a knock on his suite's door and a messenger delivered Wainwright's response. He reviewed the edits and made those changes with which he agreed accordingly. On Friday morning, Anderson was sitting next to President La Pen when he heard himself being introduced. He approached the podium to a modest round of applause.

"Ladies and Gentlemen," he began, "My name is Clint Anderson, the Governor of the State of Texas. I fully expect to become the next President of the United States. There is a development of which I want to make you aware.

"Last week, senior officials from the government of Denmark were in negotiations with a delegation from the People's Republic of China. There were two principal subjects. The first was the building of exclusively Chinese docks in the port of Aarhus. This was to facilitate their container ships delivering Chinese goods to the European Union. The second was the construction of a Chinese naval base on the East Coast of Greenland. This was to both create a Chinese naval presence in the Atlantic and to monitor the GIUK gap through which NATO surface and underwater naval vessels frequently enter the Atlantic theater.

"There is no doubt, nor is there any denial on their part, that the Chinese expect to eventually control the world. They have now targeted the European Union. When you put the construction of your 5G and internet network out to bid, the Chinese rigged the game so that they could not lose.

"In doing so, they have gained control of your economies, governments, and day-to-day life. They captured your economies by selling Chinese goods, either explicitly or through dummy corporations disguised as domestic companies, and adding all of the profits to their country's bottom line. Then they hijacked your social media, controlling the messages which reached you during the course of your individual federal elections, thereby dictating their outcomes. And they have monitored your ways of life by capturing not only your telephone calls, emails, and text messages but hacking into any active webcam tied into the internet. That means any camera from traffic cams to catch speeders to cameras monitoring the design and construction of your countries' most highly advanced weapons systems. You cannot hide from them.

"If the European Union is to survive, China must be expelled. Denmark anticipates giving China added access to their and, by extension, your countries' autonomy. When I become president, I will unilaterally impose trade sanctions upon Denmark and I would ask all of you to do the same. If the trade sanctions are not sufficient motivation to get Denmark to do the right thing, I'm going to take it a step further.

"The annual operating budget of NATO, in both direct and indirect support, is roughly $1 trillion. Of that, the United States' monetary contribution is $40 billion while the aggregate monetary contribution of the 21 member countries of the EU is less than $20 billion. I will seriously consider withholding the American contribution. Because of our technological superiority and our unique geographical circumstances, we can defend ourselves.

"Twenty-one of the twenty-seven members of the European Union are members of NATO. You have each pledged to contribute 2% of your Gross Domestic Product (GDP) to support the operations of NATO. Some of you have reached that goal while others are still struggling to do so. Without America's contribution, programs and initiatives will have to be pared down. And should the U.S. withdraw from NATO or fail to comply with Article Five of the compact, that of mutual defense, Europe will find itself in a tenuous position with respect to any incursion by Russia or, for that matter, China. I urge you to think long and hard about that contingency.

"I ask that the government of Denmark reconsider the alliance which they are contemplating with China and that the rest of you exercise whatever influence is necessary to prevent what may well be the beginning of the end of the European Union as a viable entity.

"Thank you, Ladies and Gentlemen, for taking the time to listen to my words today."

With that, Anderson took his seat. Around the auditorium there was stunned silence. Most of the delegations spoke English, so the impact of Anderson's words had been immediate. Some, however, had to wait until they heard the translators' recitations before reacting.

Prime Minister Mette Frederiksen of Denmark was beside herself. Not only had Anderson preempted her announcement but he had thoroughly raked it over the coals. Ursula von der Leyen, the President of the European Commission, had taken to the podium and was repeatedly banging her gavel to try to bring some order to the auditorium.

Eventually, the uproar calmed down enough for her to speak.

"Ladies and Gentlemen. LADIES and GENTLEMEN!" she said. "Please take your seats so that we may proceed. In light of the content of the comments of the last speaker, I think it only prudent that we hear from Prime Minister Mette Frederiksen of Denmark. Prime Minister?"

Frederiksen gathered her papers from the desktop in front of her and slowly made her way to the podium. She placed the sheet of paper with her bullet points on top of the stack of papers. Then she cleared her throat and began to speak.

Thirty minutes later, the Prime Minister of Denmark concluded her remarks. She had planned to do a presentation on the benefits that both her country and the European Union would reap from Denmark's cooperative agreement with China. Instead, she had been forced by Anderson to place a spin on her presentation geared at defending that same cooperative agreement.

She had expected to take her seat to the applause of the gathered heads of state in the auditorium of the Europa Building. Instead, she left the stage to suspicious whispers.

Chapter Twenty-eight

Robert Allen had won the 2020 presidential election by the slimmest of margins. There had been recounts and lawsuits. But, in the end, he had been sworn in as the 46th President of the United States on January 20th, 2021.

The Covid-19 virus had come to North America in or before February 2020 on the watch of President John Jefferson. Under the Jefferson Administration, pharmaceutical companies had been prompted to develop a vaccine to combat the virus with all due haste. Jefferson had set a goal for the scientists to have a vaccine ready to go public by the end of the year and the scientists had come through.

The most difficult part of counteracting the new virus still lay ahead; that of getting the American public to accept the efficacy of the vaccine and line up for their shots. By a sheer coincidence of timing, the responsibility for distributing and administering the vaccine fell to the new president, Robert Allen. Unlike the development of the vaccine, the task of distributing and administering the vials of vaccine was badly bungled.

The American public was skeptical. Early reports spoke of serious reactions to the second dose of the two-dose vaccine regimen. And those reports were accurate.

People were told to plan on taking a few days off from work after the second shot or taking it on a Friday with the weekend to recover. In the end, the strong reaction to the second shot meant that the vaccine had done its job and that the antibodies in the bloodstream now recognized the virus and the body rallied all of its defenses to combat it. But the reaction could still be debilitating. And then there were those rare cases of anaphylactic shock. That meant that once someone received their shot, they had to wait fifteen minutes in the clinic to make sure that their bodies showed no immediate ill effects.

There were those who were skeptical of the efficacy of the vaccine and simply did not take it. There were others who sought religious exemptions from having to get the shots. There were those who were simply afraid of shots. And, finally, there were those who did not accept the government telling them what to do.

Under the Allen Administration, prompting evolved into mandates. There were those who were forced to get the shots or lose their jobs, including federal employees, healthcare workers, and members of the armed forces. And because of the dubious value of the additional requirements to wear a mask and maintain "social distance", many people were either fired or just quit their jobs.

Restaurants were closed, shoppers stopped shopping, factories were shuttered, and the economy went to Hell.

Because daycare centers were closed, at least one parent in each family with young children had to stay at home. And in one-parent families that meant that there was no income.

The federal government responded by supplementing state unemployment checks with federal funds. It was a short-term, but not well thought out, solution. As the virus died down, many people just didn't return to work. Some because their jobs no longer existed, but others because they were bringing in more money on unemployment than they could otherwise earn. The economy devolved further.

Then to make matters even worse, with the American means of production shut down and the economy slowing down even further with many individuals and families having no disposable income, retail sales of consumer goods collapsed. The only consumer goods available were those being imported. And the country that imported the most consumer goods to America was China. They were more than happy to take the Americans' money, but the demand caused backlogs at the West Coast docks and the supply chain was further crippled by the shortage of long-haul truck drivers.

The final disastrous policy decision of the Allen Administration was the American military withdrawal from the twenty-year war in Afghanistan. Jefferson had planned to leave behind a token "peacekeeping" force to prevent the violent Taliban regime from retaking control of the country.

But Allen simply withdrew all the troops, leaving much of the military hardware behind. It was hard enough to evacuate the embassy staff in the capital of Kabul. But other Americans, including students and families, as well as Afghanis who had assisted the American military, were just left behind. The lucky ones were able to make it out with the assistance of private groups, many of them organized by veterans of the Afghanistan War. Many remained stranded.

Going into the 2024 presidential election, Allen had little going for him and terrible poll numbers. And his Vice President was no more beloved. The Democrat Party went through the ritual of a convention but, as with most presidents running for a second term, Allen received the nomination as the party had not had the forethought to raise a new generation of viable leaders. And, as he had predicted, Texas Governor Clint Anderson took the Republican nomination in a virtual "walkover", to use a wrestling term.

The campaigns were short, the conventions having taken place late and the campaigning being done for the most part "virtually", as were the conventions, on television and the internet because of the lingering fears of the transmission of Covid-19. As expected, Anderson won in a landslide. The impact of his victory hit the European Union hard.

Prime Minister Mette Frederiksen had gone ahead

with the deal negotiated by her ministers with China. The construction of the Chinese port facilities in Aarhus was well underway as was the construction of the naval base on the East Coast of Greenland. It was as though either no member of the Danish delegation at the EU General Assembly at which Anderson had spoken had believed him *or* that no one had given him a chance of winning the presidency. Neither had turned out to be a good bet.

The 2022 mid-term elections had gone just as the Republicans had hoped they would. By flipping about a dozen seats from Blue to Red, the party had seized control of the House of Representatives. The 50 – 50 tie in the Senate, with the Vice President able to break tie votes and throw them to the Democrats, was eliminated by a decisive win by the Republicans as they took a 55 – 45 majority into the presidential election year.

Consequently, shortly afternoon January 20th, 2025, when Clint Anderson was inaugurated as the 47th President of the United States, bills were introduced in both the House and the Senate to put some of Anderson's preferred domestic and foreign policies into law. Ironically, on Inauguration Day one of the first acts of President Anderson was not as momentous as that of other presidents. Customarily, the incoming president signs a large number of Executive Orders to undo those Executive Orders which had been signed into law by the preceding president of the other party. But this time there were few to undo.

President Allen, upon taking office, had undone the vast majority of Executive Orders signed into law by President John Jefferson. But he had so ineptly managed the country that he found that Jefferson's orders had actually been well thought out and in the best interests of the country. Sheepishly, and to no fanfare by the liberal media, he had reinstated many of the policies in Jefferson's Executive Orders. Thus, there were far fewer than usual to rescind.

Near the top of the list of new bills which Anderson had had his Republican colleagues in the House and Senate introduce were ones that would impose economic sanctions on Denmark for having gone through with their agreement to permit China to construct docking facilities in Aarhus for their own exclusive use and the development of a naval installation on the East Coast of Greenland to create a Chinese presence in the Atlantic and to monitor the GIUK Gap.

There was the usual amount of debate on the bills in both houses of Congress. The Democrats protested that the Danes had historically been loyal allies of the Americans. And the Republicans did not contradict them. But they were looking at the larger picture. If China could pick off one member of the European Union, why not a second for some other initiative? No, they had to be stopped now before their foothold in Europe included the likes of Germany or the United Kingdom.

Chapter Twenty-nine

No sooner had the trade sanction bills against Denmark been filed than staffers in both houses of Congress with connections to China transmitted the text of them to Wang Wentao, the Minister for Commerce, in Beijing. Subsequently, Wang forwarded the texts to the office of President Xi Jinping. In response, Xi called a meeting of Wang, Wang Yi, Minister of Foreign Affairs, and General Wei Fenghe, the Minister of National Defense, the three diplomats who had negotiated the agreement on their trip to Copenhagen. They would meet the first thing the following Monday morning around the conference table in President Xi's large but austere office in Zhongnanhai, China's red-walled leadership compound in Beijing.

When the four men met, Xi handed out a copy of the transcript of President Anderson's speech from the European Union General Assembly to each of them. He asked them to read it carefully and provided five minutes of total silence so that they could concentrate on each word.

Even as the four men were meeting in Beijing, reports were pouring in from Chinese embassies and consulates throughout the member states of the European Union and NATO that their legislative bodies were drafting legislation to impose trade sanctions upon Denmark until such time as they nullified their agreement with China regarding both the port facilities in Aarhus and the naval base on Greenland. Because it would be both disrespectful and disruptive to interrupt President Xi's meeting each time a new report arrived, they were periodically hand-carried into the meeting in batches. The stack of papers on the conference table was growing by the hour.

"We must stop this madness," yelled Xi. "We made Denmark a legitimate offer which promised to be profitable for them and they accepted. The fact that it is also beneficial to us, both economically and militarily, should be of no concern to any of these countries who are drafting legislation. We must get our best propagandists working on social media posts which oppose these sanctions against Denmark under the guise of local political organizations." All three heads around the table nodded.

"Next, I want the three of you on a plane to Copenhagen before the sun sets tonight. Wang," said Xi, referring to the Foreign Minister, "I want you to get on the phone to Ambassador Feng in Denmark as soon as you leave this office and have him reassemble the three ministers with whom you met previously for a follow-up meeting. The sooner the better.

"Finally, if necessary we may have to come up with some provisions whereby we can sweeten the pot for Denmark. I want each of you to be thinking up offers in your own realm which might soften the blow of the sanctions if we fail to fend them off. As you come up with ones I want you to have them transmitted to me personally. I will evaluate them and respond. But do not extend any offers before I have explicitly approved them.

"I'll have my Executive Assistant contact the crew at Daxing Airport and have them ready one of our Tupolev Tu-154s for your flight. This meeting is terminated. You have a trip to take and work to do. As for me, I will meet with my trusted advisors and let them know of our plan. Should they have any constructive input, I will share it with you in my response to your transmissions. Good day, Gentlemen."

* * *

Before the Chinese airliner had even arrived at Kastrup Airport in Copenhagen, social media had been flooded with posts from nearly every seemingly local political interest group in Europe. They had, of course, virtually all originated in China. The European Union had become a model of socialism and the thought of China as an enemy was a foreign concept. If China wanted to do something in the interests of Denmark and Denmark was, in return, willing to do something in the interests of China, why should anyone object, or interfere?

But there was a subliminal agenda afoot of which the average European man on the street was totally unaware. China was in the process of driving a wedge between

Europe and the United States. American buying power may no longer prop up the European retail markets and the American military may no longer feel obliged to support, much less bail out, the European military should an assault come from either Russia or China.

It was with these factors in mind that the three diplomats from China would be meeting with their counterparts from Denmark at the Chinese Embassy in Hellerup. When the three representatives of the Danish government arrived at the embassy in the morning, they were greeted with the same warmth which they had enjoyed on their first trip to Hellerup. It was as though nothing negative had transpired.

When they convened in the dining room to commence their talks, it was Foreign Minister Wang, the leader of the Chinese delegation, who spoke first.

"Gentlemen, and Lady, I wish to start out by expressing our appreciation for you accommodating our request for a follow-up meeting on such short notice. This speech by this Anderson fellow from America seems to have ruffled some feathers among your colleagues from the European Union and NATO.

"To me," he continued, "the problem is not so much in what he said but how he spun it in such a way as to make our agreement sound threatening to either of these two respected institutions. A threat was neither intended nor expressed. Our agreement was simply a business transaction between two autonomous nations; nothing more.

"The thought that it posed any sort of threat to the continent of Europe is ludicrous. What is good for Denmark is, by extension, good for Europe. Your prosperity contributes to Europe's prosperity."

"But the feedback we have received from our EU and NATO colleagues, not to mention the United States," interrupted Foreign Minister Kofod, "has been universally negative. They envision China as attempting to influence, if not monopolize, the dynamics of international trade in Europe. And, as for the Chinese naval facility on Greenland, NATO, especially the United States, perceives it as a potential precursor to a naval engagement against the West in the Atlantic." Kofod could not have known at that moment just how right he was.

For the next two days, the six ministers would be meeting as a group to try and devise ways in which the Danes could defuse the outcry of their colleagues while, at the same time, coming up with ways in which the Chinese could further enhance the value of the arrangement to Denmark without compromising its utility to the Chinese.

What went undetected to the assembled diplomats were the small fleet of Swedish sedans which were rotating overwatch of the Chinese Embassy. As Denmark had no universally-recognizable domestically-manufactured automobiles, the easiest way to blend in was to drive a Volvo or Saab sedan from neighboring Sweden. Different colored Volvos and Saabs driven by different drivers would attract no attention whatsoever.

The only thing the overwatch sedans all had in common was that their drivers were universally male. Some had beards or mustaches or both. Some were clean-shaven and some somewhat scraggly as though they had worked late or slept at the office the previous night. Finally, some were dressed in business suits while others were dressed for a day on the assembly line at one of the nearby factories.

Conducting reconnaissance of the Chinese Embassy and its occupants would prove to be unexpectedly easy as none of the Chinese ministers ever left the building. On both mornings the three Danish ministers arrived within fifteen minutes of one another, each driven in their own limousine by their own driver. The reverse would occur roughly eight hours later. But they were not the subjects of the operators' attention.

On the evening of the second day, the three Chinese ministers exited the front door of the embassy and climbed into the familiar black town car. It exited through the main gate and headed for Kastrup Airport. But, this time, it had a few trailing vehicles conducting covert surveillance.

Chapter Thirty

No sooner had the bills imposing trade sanctions on Denmark been introduced on the floor of the two houses of Congress than a phone call had gone out from the office of the Chief of Naval Operations (CNO) in the Pentagon to Naval Amphibious Base Little Creek in Virginia. Little Creek and its neighboring Dam Neck Annex were the East Coast home of the U.S. Navy SEALs. The switchboard operator in Virginia had to do a little hunting before she located the Commander of SEAL Team Eight, Thomas Carlisle.

"Yes, Admiral," said Carlisle when he came on the line. "I've been awaiting your call."

"You've got your 'Go'," said the CNO and hung up.

Anyone who had spent any time in Washington knew that every government office had among its ranks those with interests other than those of the United States. Therefore, it was reasonable to assume that at least one senator and one congressman had on their staff someone with sympathies for China. And that that person would have forwarded the text of the trade sanction bills against Denmark to Beijing. All the CNO had done was to be prepared.

Carlisle called four pre-selected four-man teams from

SEAL Team Eight together in the Ward Room and briefed them on their mission. The Chinese had been negotiating with Denmark to undertake projects which would present a clear and present danger to the national security of the U.S. The three ministers from China who had negotiated those projects were returning to Denmark. The SEALs' job was to see to it that they did not return unimpeded to China, but also to maintain their health and safety.

After their briefing and a short time to gather their "Go" bags, Commander Carlisle and his sixteen SEALs boarded a Gulfstream 450 at adjacent Oceana Naval Air Station for their ride to Royal Navy Air Station Yeovilton in Southwest England. For the past week, the U.S. Navy's Carrier Strike Group Twelve with the USS *Gerald R. Ford* as its flagship had been conducting joint naval exercises with the Royal Navy at the North and South ends of the English Channel. The purpose of the exercise was to practice the surveillance and interdiction of Russian vessels which used the channel to shorten the route of vessels from their Northern Fleet headquarters in Murmansk departing the Arctic Ocean to enter the Mediterranean.

Once at Yeovilton, the SEALs would be choppered out to the *Ford* by an AgustaWestland AW101 *Merlin*. Then the fun would start. The seventeen SEALs would catch their C-2 *Greyhound*, a twin-prop, high-wing cargo aircraft to a small, private hangar in the remote FBO (fixed-base operator) section of Kastrup Airport in Copenhagen. The hangar would serve as the SEALs' base of operations while they were in Denmark.

The first thing they noticed was the small fleet of late-model Saabs and Volvos parked adjacent to the hangar on the side away from the main terminal and essentially out of sight. These would allow them to surveil any location virtually undetected and tail any vehicle by "leapfrogging" the subject so that one car was never consistently in their rearview mirror.

Once their gear was unloaded, two two-man teams hopped into two cars, one a red Volvo and the other a blue Saab, and drove to the Chinese Embassy. The Volvo parked across the street and down the block from the embassy while the other, the blue Saab, just cruised the neighborhood so that the two SEALs on board could familiarize themselves with the access and egress routes to the closest major highway.

It was just over two blocks to a major North – South highway that paralleled the main railroad trunk lines into Copenhagen. After making a left-hand turn onto the on-ramp of Highway 152 heading South, they would follow it until they reached Highway 02 which would carry them along the waterfront through Copenhagen. A left across the Nyhavn Canal, a brief right, and one last left would lead them to E20, the main access road to the airport, just under ten miles as the crow flies but more like fifteen taking the main highways.

The major tactical decision which Commander Carlisle would have to make is where to seize the Chinese diplomats. They could take them between the embassy and Highway 152, somewhere between Hellerup and Kastrup, or at the airport. Or they could take them at the airport after they exited their staff car but before they boarded their airliner.

But that brought into play a secondary consideration. The FBO facilities at the airport, though well away from the main terminal, were all in relatively close proximity to one another. That meant that the Chinese airliner was also on the tarmac there. Fortunately, the hangar housing the SEALs' *Greyhound* was a large structure. The SEALs had been able to unload what accessories they would need to conduct their operation out of sight of others at the FBO sector of the airport. In addition, any markings on the aircraft identifying it as the property of the U.S. Navy had been painted over before they boarded it.

The markings issue was not insignificant. The Chinese Tu-154 carrying the ministers had also carried a number of Special Operations troops. They were there for security, not only of the ministers but of the plane. They had kept a close eye on any new arrivals to the FBO facilities and made a determination if they posed a threat to their high-profile passengers. Consequently, not a sign of any military presence was to be seen in or around the hangar housing the SEALs' *Greyhound.*

The decision was made to take the ministers well after they departed the embassy but well before they approached the airport and its concentration of Chinese Special Operations forces. Highway 152 offered the best option with the constant flow of rail traffic providing a din of noise and its remoteness from high-density housing or offices.

On the afternoon of the second day of the meetings at the embassy, the two-vehicle deployment of Swedish surveillance sedans was supplemented by two additional vehicles. At 6:30PM, after the ministers had eaten their dinner and consumed a healthy amount of fine Western alcoholic beverages, they had boarded their staff car for the trip to the airport. Between the embassy and the ramp onto Highway 152, all four of the Americans' cars had fallen in line behind the black staff car.

As it headed South, the two Saabs and two Volvos converged on the staff car. The one in front slowed to a halt, the two on the driver's side blocked the car's escape, and the one behind it prevented it from going in reverse. As the driver reached for the car phone, one of the SEALs shot him with his Glock, killing him. Then four SEALs, two at each rear door, shot the locks with their automatics and extracted the three ministers. One each was shoved, face down, on the floor of the rear seat of one of the sedans. The entire exercise had taken less than a minute.

Shortly thereafter, a passing police car observed the black car with a dead man at the wheel. His identification showed his connection to the Chinese embassy. The police called in the discovery to their local precinct which, in turn, called the embassy. The embassy called the Special Operations commander at the airport and all but a handful departed for the embassy and staff car.

The SEALs had duct-taped the mouths of the three ministers and bound them with it at the wrists and ankles. Ironically, the four vehicles carrying the SEALs and their captives passed the trucks carrying the Chinese Special Operations troops as they approached the airport. But there was nothing out of the ordinary to be seen.

When the four SEALs vehicles reached their hangar, the ministers were hustled inside out of view of anyone else and loaded onto the *Greyhound*. All the SEALs jumped on board and, after the hangar doors were opened, the *Greyhound* taxied out to one of the shorter runways. The Chinese Special Operations troops observed the plane's departure but saw nothing unusual. The funny thing was not one of them had ever seen a *Greyhound* before.

The small plane was aloft in ten minutes, reaching its cruising altitude in five. At its cruising speed of 289 miles per hour, it would take them two hours to reach the *Ford*.

Chapter Thirty-one

The manner in which these three Chinese ministers were treated while onboard the USS *Gerald R. Ford* would have great impact upon the speed and diplomacy with which this episode would be concluded. There may have been a time when they would have simply been thrown in the brig, but those days had passed. Three of the ship's top-ranking officers gave up their private quarters, complete with "heads", for the ministers. First, each of them opened their safes and removed all materials and placed them in the master safe on the bridge. Next they "sanitized" their quarters of any documents which had the potential to reveal anything about the ship, its mission, or its capabilities.

The ministers were shown to the Ward Room and seated at the conference table. They were each given a cup of hot tea in the Captain's china, asked if they were hungry, and made as comfortable as one could be in one's adversary's most powerful naval vessel. The ship's captain, Captain Michael Wentworth, and the commander of Carrier Strike Group Twelve, Rear Admiral Gregory C. Huffman, entered the room and sat at either end of the conference table.

A translator had accompanied the ship's two highest-ranking officers. He sat across the table from the ministers. When all were seated and comfortable, the dialogue commenced. Admiral Huffman would be the first to speak. He had received authorization from the President by way of the National Security Council and the State Department to initiate negotiations.

"Gentlemen," he began, "My name is Admiral Gregory Huffman. I am the commander of Carrier Strike Group Twelve, the flagship of which you are currently aboard. The President of the United States has authorized me to engage you in a discussion, the purpose of which is to have the Peoples' Republic of China release control of the new port facilities in Aarhus, Denmark, and to abandon what work has been conducted on the new Chinese naval base in Greenland."

"Under what authority do you claim the right to make such demands?" asked Foreign Minister Wang.

"My purpose is twofold. With respect to the port in Aarhus, you have used surveillance, eavesdropping, coercion, and money to entice an ally of the United States to act in a way contrary to the best interests of its fellow members of the European Union, my country, and itself. As for the naval base, our National Security Council, with the concurrence of President Anderson, has declared that it represents a 'clear and present danger' to the national security of the United States. By that I mean that the mere presence of an enemy naval stronghold in the middle of the Atlantic Ocean is 'of such a nature as to create a clear and present danger that [it] . . . will bring about [a] . . . substantive [evil] that [the] Congress [of the United States] has a right to prevent.' In consultation with Congress, the President, at the advice of the National Security Council, has deemed that the construction of such a military installation could well be a precursor to an attack by the PRC on the interest and homeland of either the United States or one of its NATO allies.

"Your own government," said Huffman, "has filed similar claims with the United Nations against several nations on the Pacific Rim and in the Indo-Pacific theater. We anticipate exercising that exact same right."

"But you have not taken such action to date," protested Wang.

"The paperwork is being filed as we speak," responded Huffman. "And, as for the naval base, even now it poses an imminent threat to the safety and well-being of the United States and its NATO allies."

"But you have taken me and my two colleagues as hostages on one of your naval vessels," said Wang. "Surely this constitutes an act of war!"

"We view this as an act of diplomacy," said Huffman. "The loss of the life of your driver was regrettable. We intend to make full reparations for that act to you and your country. But while your movement has been restricted, you have all been treated well, housed in quarters equal to those of the senior naval officers aboard this vessel, and you will be returned to the location of your choice once this episode has concluded. We saw little short of these actions, and avoided a much greater military engagement, if we had been required to bring about the same ends by means of force. What we ask of you is your release of Denmark from its current obligations and China's withdrawing its incursion into the digital infrastructure of the European Union.

"We know full well that the three of you cannot commit China to our demands on your own authority. This ship possesses the ability to communicate with anyone anywhere in the world. We will have three telephones brought to this conference room. We will put you in touch with whomever you wish. But, be advised that we will be recording all incoming and outgoing communications. Goodwill will have to be earned."

"Admiral Huffman," asked Wang, "can you please leave me and my two colleagues alone for a while so that we might discuss among ourselves how it is that we will proceed?"

"We will grant you your request," replied Huffman, "But be aware that your discussion, as with your outgoing communications, will be being monitored. I strongly suggest that you use your relative privacy to speak frankly to one another with the goal of bringing this unfortunate incident to a conclusion."

"Very well," said Wang. "Please leave us for now so that we may devise a plan whereby we might fulfill your demands in conformance with the wishes and requirements of our superiors."

"This room is yours for as long as it takes. There will be two Marine guards just outside the door. Should you need anything, simply knock on the door. One of them will respond and pass any requests, be it for drink, food, a return to your rooms, or any other reasonable accommodation, on to me. Upon my approval, your request will be fulfilled."

With that, Admiral Huffman and Captain Wentworth exited the room and the three Chinese ministers began their mutual consultations. But before the admiral and captain had left the Ward Room, Foreign Minister Wang had asked for a fresh pot of tea. It would not be one of the exotic Da Hong Pao blends which dated back to the Ming dynasty and were served in the halls of the Zhongnanhai compound in Beijing but rather Darjeeling. They would have to make do.

Once the fresh pot of tea had been brought in and three hot cups poured, the ministers set about their work. As the senior of the three, Foreign Minister Wang was the first to speak.

"Gentlemen," Wang began, "It is clear that the Americans are aware of the steps which our country has taken to insinuate ourselves and our political philosophies into the daily lives of the citizens of the European Union. Moreover, they have also seen through our devious efforts at misleading the Danes in entering into an agreement that gave us both an economic and military foothold in the heart of the European Union and its neighboring allies. If we so desire, we may protest and deny these claims, but it would only buy time and not result in any final resolution of this matter.

"I suggest that we each contact our superiors in Beijing and tell them of our current circumstances. They cannot fail to see the futility in drawing out this ordeal any longer than necessary. And it will get us home in the shortest amount of time."

"Not so fast," replied General Wei Fenghe, the Minister of National Defense. "For years, President Xi has sought to gain the right to establish a naval base on the Atlantic, either along the West Coast of Africa or on an island at sea. We have, on his behalf, negotiated the construction of just such a base. He will not willingly or easily forfeit that great military inroad.

"America's President Anderson warned the European Union of the consequences which they would incur if we were allowed to undertake just the advances which are now coming to fruition. Do not suppose that President Xi will back down just to save our lives or prevent the three of us from having to live out our lives in captivity. He will see it as but a small price to pay for the superiority it provides.

"We must learn of just what the reaction of the other EU nations has been to our capture and to the resolutions which the United States has filed with the United Nations. If they oppose them, then President Xi may wish to see how this gambit plays itself out. It may be that the United States may have to go it alone and act solely in its own best interests. Should that be the case, what momentarily appears to be an economic and military loss for China could well turn into a glorious diplomatic victory for ourselves and our nation." It was now time for Wang Wentao, the Minister for Commerce, to speak.

"We have lost sight of the original premise for our undertaking," said Wang. "This entire endeavor began a few years ago with the goal of China constructing a 5G network in the European Union. Using that as our weapon, we could capture the hearts and minds of the EU citizenry. Our propagandists were quite wily in their use of social media in the EU to mold the majority of European leadership into a body that would no longer view China as a threat but rather as an ideological ally. We have achieved that goal.

"Additionally, the port facilities in Aarhus and the naval base on Greenland will give us the tools to

197

subversively manipulate the economic environment and balance of military power of a good portion of the European continent. That is not a position which President Xi would readily give up. We must speak with our peers and superiors to learn of the reactions of the EU countries and their leaders to our capture.

"The European Union may rebel at this gesture of the United States. In that case, President Xi will surely refuse to comply with the Americans' demands. Only if the EU sees what has truly happened to them will they firmly align themselves with the United States. And, at such a time, President Xi will have to decide what is to become of us."

Wang had convinced his colleagues. Foreign Minister Wang went to the door of the Ward Room and knocked. A Marine responded. He told him that he and the two other ministers would be making phone calls and that they would wish not to be disturbed. The Marine closed the door and passed the message on to Captain Wentworth. The Captain called Admiral Huffman and told him what the Chinese' plans were. Huffman concurred.

The word was passed back to the Marine who knocked on the Ward Room door. Foreign Minister Wang answered it and was told of Admiral Huffman's reply. The three men then began to call those in Beijing with whom they would have to consult. The tone of the calls began as outrage but slowly evolved into one of deviousness.

Chapter Thirty-two

The three Chinese ministers were soon on the phone to their home offices in Beijing. They were quite aware that their every word was being monitored, so they were limited to speaking of things of which they knew the Americans were well aware. Nonetheless, they could accomplish a great deal by using not only their intellect but their cunning.

Foreign Minister Wang called the headquarters of the Ministry of Foreign Affairs. He asked to speak with Le Yucheng, his Executive Vice-Minister. After assuring him that he was well but that he was being detained by the Americans, he got right down to business.

"Minister Le," Wang began, "The most important thing you can do to assist me is to test the waters and obtain the reaction of heads of state and opinion leaders around the world, but focused upon the European Union and the former Eastern Bloc countries, to the actions which the Americans have undertaken by taking me, General Wei, and Minister Wang as virtual hostages. Most of them will have made statements which can be found in the world press or their own nation's newspapers or websites. Some will be predictable while others are currently unpredictable by me.

"In France, President Le Pen's support for the actions taken by America's President Anderson is to be totally expected. She is a far Right-Wing politician and both she and Anderson share the same conservative world view. But we will not be dictated to by Right-Wingers. Now the effectiveness of our propagandists at home on the citizenry and politicians in the European Union's capitals will become apparent and show their work's worth. With their support, we may well prevail.

"President Anderson and the United States will not want to stand virtually alone in the eyes of the European Union. They could well choose to do so, but there will be a price to be paid. However, if the support from the EU capitals is nearly universally positive, they may well persist in this folly. I want you to do your homework and then contact me with a summary of your findings." When Wang was done, he provided Le with the manner in which he could be contacted and then set him about his work.

General Wei had called the office of Admiral Miao Hua, the Director of the Political Work Department of the Central Military Commission. There were always two types of military leaders; warrior generals and political generals. As was apparent from his title, Miao was a political general or, in this case, admiral.

"Admiral Miao," said General Wei when the connection was completed, "As you must know by now, I have been taken prisoner by the Americans. Our release will only be achieved by Denmark reneging upon their agreement with us regarding the port facilities in Aarhus and our naval base on Greenland. To allow me to best advise President Xi as to my recommendation for how China should respond to America's outlandish actions, I will need to know the current state of military affairs among the United States, the several nations of the European Union, and those European nations that are not members of the EU.

"The best way of assessing that state is by taking an inventory of their troop movements and fleet deployments. Before I go further, or before you say anything at all, I must tell you that any communication between you and me will be monitored by the Americans, be it here on board this aircraft carrier or by their intelligence community back in Washington. So be very guarded in what you say.

"We, as with all developed countries, have numerous ways of collecting the information to which I just alluded. First, there are the satellites that can provide us with the 'big picture' of troop movements and fleet deployments. Second, our new Xi'an KJ-600 reconnaissance aircraft can provide us with more precise information with its side-looking airborne radar (SLAR), as well as signals intelligence (SIGINT), by flying in international airspace adjacent to a nation's autonomous airspace. Finally, there are our sources of human intelligence, or HUMINT. But you must report that to me, if indeed it even exists, in such a way that those listening in on us cannot identify the source of that intelligence. We've spent years getting those men, *and women*, in positions of authority with access to classified troop movement and fleet deployment information. We cannot afford to provide those listening in on us with any hint as to where those informants are stationed. That must be avoided at all costs.

"Do your best to give me an accurate picture of today's strategic situation. I want to know where all European Union and NATO forces are deployed, as well as those of non-NATO European countries, so that I may deduce the allegiances of all of the actors. Only then can I best advise our superior, President Xi Jinping.

"I will be expecting to hear from you in short order. Foreign Minister Wang must keep President Xi informed and make his recommendations as to how China should react to our capture. The less aggressive the movements of the EU nations are, the more inclined he may be to wait this protracted gesture out and call the American's bluff. He will see our lives as a small price to pay for hegemony on the European continent."

"I understand," replied Vice-Minister Le. "Both my best men and I will get on it right away. I will call back with a comprehensive report which the Americans could no doubt come up with on their own but without which President Xi will be unable to make an informed decision."

"Thank you, Vice-Minister. I will look forward to

hearing from you when you have your report compiled," said Wei. "I will then share your information with both Minister Wang and President Xi. Your efforts will not go unnoticed or unrewarded."

"I understand," said Le. "You will not be disappointed."

"Very well, then," replied Wei. "Goodbye."

Of the three ministers' phone calls, one would have assumed that Minister Wang Wentao's would have been thought to be the least critical. But what he would find would be integral to President Xi's decisions. This undertaking was, in part, about international economics and China's ability to influence them. Wang's findings would play a crucial role in dictating this episode's outcome.

Wang called Chen Jian, the Director of the Department of Foreign Economic Cooperation. His request was rather simple relative to his two colleagues. All Wang asked of Chen was to be kept apprised of the movements of the world's major economic markets. Starting at the International Dateline, those included the Tokyo Stock Exchange (the Nikkei Index), the Shanghai Stock Exchange (the Shanghai Composite), the Seoul Stock Exchange (the Korea Composite Stock Price Index (KOSPI)), the London Stock Exchange (the Financial Times Stock Exchange (FTSE) Index), and the New York Stock Exchange (the Dow

Jones Industrial).

Because economics was one of the driving forces in China's bid to capture the European Union's contract to build their 5G network, the movement of the world's markets in response to the capture of the three ministers would help dictate President Xi's future decisions. The request was simple; daily updates on the world's indices.

Director Chen's answer was simple. "You'll have them."

When the three ministers' phone calls were complete, Foreign Minister Wang went to the door and summoned one of the Marine guards. He told him that he and his colleagues would like to eat and then be returned to their rooms for their first sleep in a protracted number of hours. The request was approved by Admiral Huffman and breakfast brought in.

As the three ministers were dining, they informed one another of the information they had solicited from their subordinates. They were all in agreement that that the sum total of the information requested, when digested and submitted to President Xi, would provide him with the facts he would need to respond to their being taken captive.

After they had dined, they returned to their quarters. Foreign Minister Wang asked the Marine guard if they could please be informed of any calls after they had gone to bed.

Chapter Thirty-three

Chinese bureaucrats in Beijing were going about the tasks they had been given by their ministers while military intelligence operatives around the world worked to collect the information with which they had been tasked. At the same time, diplomats from American embassies and consulates across the face of the Earth were fanning out to promote President Anderson's policies and agenda. It was unlikely that, at least in some foreign capitals, the Chinese and American emissaries had not crossed paths in the performance of their respective duties.

Secretary of State Wainwright had made it clear to his ambassadors and Foreign Service Officers (FSOs) that the preferred, and preferably peaceful, resolution of this diplomatic stalemate would only be possible with their best efforts. The key to this strategy was not to convince foreign leaders that the agenda was in America's best interest but that it was in their own. Only when a leader was convinced that a decision was in his own country's best interest would they consider incorporating it into their nation's policies.

However, regardless of a head of state's personal beliefs, each had a constituency which had to be convinced of a decision being in their best interests. Otherwise, a head of state would be a one-term leader. And any politician's first priority, after being elected, was to get re-elected.

Consequently, everyone from presidents to prime ministers was going out to promote President Anderson's agenda to their populace. When it came to diplomacy, money talked. And Anderson's policies with respect to finances would enrich the bottom line of the subject country at the expense of China.

American diplomats in Europe, especially in the European Union and most notably in Denmark, were spending hours, if not days, meeting with the local politicians. There were concessions that the United States was prepared to make with a given government that would not appear on the front page of *The New York Times*, *The Washington Post*, or the local press. In the end, however, the vast majority of nations saw their way to supporting President Anderson's policies and agenda.

The details of the deals which America was prepared to cut with a given government were not the sort of information which a Chinese ambassador, diplomat, or bureaucrat could readily obtain. All that they could determine was that the sentiments of government leaders in Europe appeared to be leaning in the United States' direction, even if the predominant political persuasion of the head of state did not always coincide with the American president. As loyal party members, one and all, those sent into the field to take the pulse of the national leaders would be reluctant to report their findings back to Beijing. But report they must.

When word of the trend reached President Xi, he was furious. The Chinese government had subsidized the installation of the EU nations' 5G network to give their propagandists access to their citizenry and, as a result, influence their choices of leaders. Moreover, they could capture a larger segment of the consumer goods market by advertising their products on social media under the guise of domestic products. And, finally, they could use the communications and images as a source of intelligence. This had all gone wrong.

The ploy of negotiating with Denmark to establish exclusively Chinese port facilities and gain a foothold in the Atlantic by establishing a naval base on Greenland had antagonized the Americans beyond their level of tolerance. The U.S. had weighed in using their overwhelming political influence and leverage over Western economies to exert influence on the EU's heads of state. And, if that was not enough, they had threatened to throw the world's balance of military power out of control by using NATO as their weapon of choice.

Xi had used his high-ranking leaders as his emissaries to negotiate with Denmark. But they were not the most powerful men in their respective disciplines. Those men had names that were not widely spoken outside the halls of power or known to be within Xi's inner circle. But they could help influence decisions while being accountable to no one. They were the men Xi now called upon.

Sometimes one by one, sometimes in groups, these men were brought into obscure meeting rooms in the Forbidden City within the Dongcheng District of Beijing. There, they would meet with President Xi. The range of options they discussed as to how to deal with Washington was not repeated outside those rooms because the Xi Administration would insist upon maintaining plausible deniability in the event any of them were carried out.

If a high-ranking American political leader were to fall ill or suffer a fatal accident, it could be attributed to bad luck. If a hypersonic missile were to strike a strategic target in the United States and disintegrate its target and itself, it could be attributed to a military test gone wrong. Or if a virulent virus was to spread across North America which had never been seen in the Western Hemisphere before, it could be characterized as a rogue, mutant variant of an otherwise familiar disease.

These and many more options were discussed and dismissed. But some ideas lingered. And then, of course, there was the straightforward military approach. Because of its geographic barriers and relative isolation, a movement of ground troops or even a fusillade of missiles would never knock the United States out. But the U.S. had allies, some of them whose relationships were "special", bordering on sacred. What level of "threat" would they have to be exposed to before the United States conceded defeat? All options were on the table.

While the politicians played their "what if" games, the Peoples Liberation Army, by means of its Second Department, the intelligence division within its General Staff Headquarters, was collecting just the information General Wei had requested. Its internal classified publication, *Movements of Foreign Armies*, was published every 10 days and transmitted to units at the division level. The PLA's Institute of International Relations at Nanjing comes under the Second Department of the General Staff Headquarters and is responsible for training military attaches, assistant military attaches, and associate military attaches as well as secret agents to be posted abroad. It also supplies officers to the military intelligence sections of various military regions and group armies. The Institute was formed from the PLA "793" Foreign Language Institute which moved from Zhangjiakou after the Cultural Revolution and split in two.

The Institute of International Relations was known in the 1950s as the School for Foreign Language Cadres of the Central Military Commission, with the current name being used since 1964. The training of intelligence personnel is one of several activities at the Institute. While all graduates of the Moscow Institute of International Relations were employed by the KGB, only some graduates of the Beijing Institute of International Relations were employed by the

Ministry of State Security. The former Institute of International Relations, since renamed the Foreign Affairs College, is under the administration of the Ministry of Foreign Affairs and is not involved in secret service work. The former Central Military Commission foreign language school had foreign faculty members who were either Communist Party sympathizers or were members of foreign communist parties. But the present Institute of International Relations does not hire foreign teachers to avoid the danger that its students might be recognized when they are sent abroad as clandestine agents.

Those engaged in professional work in military academies under the Second Department of the PLA General Staff Headquarters usually have a chance to go abroad, either for advanced studies or as military officers working in the military attache's office of Chinese embassies in foreign countries. People working in the military attache's office of embassies are usually engaged in collecting military information under the cover of "military diplomacy". As long as they refrain from directly subversive activities, they are considered as well-behaved "military diplomats".

Operatives from all the applicable units were assessing the troop movements and fleet deployments of both the United States and its allies. And there were "wild cards' like India. Their relationship with the United States growing out of their, and America's, colonial past with the United Kingdom could not be discounted.

Chapter Thirty-four

The easiest data to collect, though frequently the hardest to interpret, was the economic temperament of the world. Director Chen of the Department of Foreign Economic Cooperation was carrying out his orders from Minister Wang of the Ministry of Commerce. On a daily basis, he would collect the opening and closing numbers on financial market indices around the world.

The Nikkei was holding strong as Japan was a close ally of the United States and they provided some of the high-tech components that went into American military equipment. And although it had had its rocky moments, the interpersonal relation between President Anderson and Japan's new head of state has remained both cordial and stable.

The Korea Composite Stock Price Index, or KOSPI, tended to mirror New York's Dow Jones Industrial Average. This was because the Korean economy was so integrally enmeshed with that of the United States. And other than the occasional flare-up in North Korea or temper tantrum by Kim Jong Un, the large presence of American military troops and their state-of-the-art weapons on Korean soil ensured a stability which they would not have otherwise enjoyed.

The Financial Times Stock Exchange Index, or FTSE, from the London Stock Exchange was an anomaly. Since the United Kingdom was no longer a member of the European Union, one would have expected that its performance and that of the EU's economy would no longer be related. But that was not the case. Of course, there were bumps in the road when it came to such issues as the licensing of EU pharmaceuticals in England or the perennially problematic issue of the border between Northern Ireland (part of the United Kingdom) and the Republic of Ireland (a member of the EU), but the UK and EU were still dependent upon one another in the realm of international trade. The FTSE was, more often than not, a good bellwether indicator for the strength of the EU's economy.

And then there was the Dow Jones Industrial Average. Not only was it representative of the American industrial and financial industry economy, but it was frequently taken as a surrogate for capitalism around the world. President Anderson put great stock in this and took great pride in its performance since his coming to office. None of the aforementioned indices had tanked since the American capture of the three Chinese ministers.

The significant exception to this trend, however, was the Shanghai Composite, the indicator for the Shanghai Stock Exchange and, by extension, the economy of the Peoples' Republic of China. There were some major components of the index which were dragging it down. And some of them were directly impacted by what was going on in Denmark and onboard the *Ford*.

First and foremost, there was the telecom and electronic gadgets industry. The two principal companies that had built the European Union's 5G network were Huawei and ZTE. With President Anderson's exposure of the Chinese government's genuine agenda for the use of their equipment, the value of their stock had plummeted in the world's capitalist economies.

Not far behind had been Foxconn. A company little known beyond "geekdom", Foxconn had played a pivotal role in the PRC's economy's reversal in the late 1990s and after the turn of the millennium. In 2001, Foxconn introduced the "iPod", a revolutionary .mp3 music file player. For all intents and purposes, Apple built an entire city to accommodate both the iPod factory and house its employees.

If someone in the United States sat down at their computer at sunrise on day one and ordered an iPod with custom engraving such as their name, that iPod in its shiny silver metal case would arrive at their front door within 72 hours. Imagine the responsiveness of everyone from the worker on the production line to the worker running the engraving machine to the truck driver who delivered it to the airport to the airline that delivered it to the customer's hometown. It boggles the mind and puts the Manhattan Project to shame.

In 2007 came the iPhone. It became *the* cell phone to have. It introduced all the new features which other companies' phones would eventually have. And, once again, Foxconn was the manufacturer. There was a new model introduced nearly every year once the production line and the Apple engineers got in the swing of things.

Finally, in 2010, there was the iPad, the size of an Amazon Kindle e-reader which was more powerful than many laptops more than four times the size. Soon many people who had been walking down the sidewalk staring at the tiny screens on their iPhones could now walk down that same sidewalk staring at the screen of a device they could actually read! And it was all thanks to Apple and their Chinese manufacturer, Foxconn.

Well, the world had finally learned what the Chinese had done with the likes of Huawei and ZTE. They had tried to take over the economy of the European Union by stealth. And they had been caught in the act. The economy of the electronics industry in China had plummeted and with it its stocks. That was the first drag on the Shanghai Composite.

The next would be the nation's shipbuilding industry. China produces immense ships, be they container ships or military vessels, at a rate with which no other country on

Earth can compete. The largest number of Ultra Large Container Vessels, or ULCVs, like the Maersk Triple E class which can carry 18,000 20-foot containers, are manufactured in China, South Korea, and Japan. Moreover, China's shipyards are building new warships at a rate that the United States cannot match. Their naval superiority is imminent if it has not already been reached.

But the orders for those container ships bound for Aarhus in the near future had been suspended pending the outcome of the current stalemate. And those suspended orders had taken a toll on the stock prices of China's primary shipbuilders. That put another drag on the Shanghai Composite.

And then there were the innumerable consumer goods. All of a sudden, a significant segment of the population of the European Union that had been shopping online found that the items they had been purchasing were coming from Chinese dummy corporations that had only set up a mailing address in their country. Soon they were buying their jeans, their sneakers, even their toys from genuine domestic companies. Even though they may have had to pay more or buy fewer, they knew that their expenditures were going into their own country's economy. So the dummy corporations folded, and with it went their, and their country's, profits.

The net effect of these three sectors of China's economy being hit hard by the United States' revelations and the concomitant ill will was a precipitous drop in its bottom line and with it the Shanghai Composite index. Director Chen took this all in, added it to his reports on the other indices, and contacted Minister Wang aboard the *Ford*.

It had been two weeks since Chen and Wang had spoken. Chen had nothing but bad news to deliver, but he had a job to do. When Wang came on the line, Chen began his report. Wang hadn't been sure whether he would get good news or bad news, but he had never imagined that all of the capitalist economies' indices would be going up while only China's would be tanking.

"How can this be?" asked Wang when Chen had completed his report.

Chen informed him that Beijing had underestimated America's influence upon the world's economy by its threatened sanctions and its implied threat against its support of NATO.

"But we are so much bigger," insisted Wang. "We have a larger economy and have all but captured certain segments of the world's economy; computer chips, container ships, etc. The United States cannot compete. Yet they think they can cripple our economy!" Then he hung up.

There were two more reports to come. This would not go well. And no one would want to give Xi the bad news.

Chapter Thirty-five

The next report to come in would be for General Wei from Admiral Miao, the Director of the Political Work Department of the Central Military Commission. His resources had included aerial photography from satellites, radar and signals intelligence from Xi'an KJ-600 reconnaissance aircraft, and spies on the ground. When the phone call came, General Wei took it with trepidation based upon the briefing Minister Wang had received.

"General Wei," said Miao, "I have had my people do a worldwide survey of troop movements and fleet deployments. The most activity has been from our own Navy, but that you would have already presumed. They are positioning themselves for possible defensive measures."

"Why defensive?" asked Wei.

"Because the Western navies, as well as those of Japan, Australia, and even Taiwan, have taken up positions to inflict damage on both our military forces abroad and at sea as well as the homeland itself," responded Miao.

"Tell me more, Admiral Miao," said Wei. "I must write this down."

"First, the American Navy has deployed a component

217

of its Second Fleet out of Norfolk, Virginia, Carrier Strike Force Eight headed by the aircraft carrier *Harry S. Truman*, to the North Atlantic where they have taken up a position just off the East Coast of Greenland where our new naval base and its entire contingent of naval vessels is ported. It appears that if we make a wrong move, that base will take the brunt of the American retaliation."

"While I am offended by their nerve," said Wei, "it is a typical American move."

"The Americans have also deployed Carrier Strike Group Ten, headed by the *George H. W. Bush*, also out of the Second Fleet, to the Western end of our 'Polar Silk Road'. That has effectively closed off our entrance or exit from the Atlantic into or out of the Arctic Ocean. To complement that move, they have deployed Carrier Strike Group Five headed by the *Ronald Reagan*, a component of their Seventh Fleet based in Yokosuka, Japan, to the Eastern end of the Polar Silk Road off the Russian Far East, also known as Siberia, in the Bering Strait.

"Their next move was to interdict any naval military traffic along the 'Belt' portion of our Belt and Road Initiative. They have placed warships in the South China Sea, the Strait of Malacca, both ends of the Suez Canal, and the Strait of Gibraltar.

"Finally, they have deployed semicircular rings of

ships to the East of our three fleet bases, Qingdao for our North Sea Fleet, Dinghai for our East Sea Fleet, and Zhan Jiang for our South Sea Fleet. They have essentially bottled up our entire Navy where they sit." With that, Miao completed his report on the American Navy.

"As for the rest of the Atlantic, naval ships from every European country bordering the sea have been deployed to defend their respective coasts. And in the Pacific, naval ships from Taiwan, Japan, and Australia have been deployed to occupy and patrol the Strait of Taiwan. That completes my reports on naval activity."

"I do not take what you have said lightly," said Wei, "But I do commend you on the comprehensiveness of your report. Now, tell me about troop movements."

"Because none of the nations involved in this dispute share borders with China, there have been no significant troop movements," said Miao. "The only troop activity of note is that on our border with India, but that activity predates this conflict.

"Finally, because of the access to air-to-air refuelings, no enemy aircraft have been repositioned. But each aircraft carrier carries with it its own small air force and the Americans have several long-range bombers, B-52 *Stratofortresses*, B1-B *Lancers*, and B-2 *Spirits,* based in Guam which could reach the Chinese mainland if needed."

"This is all very distressing," said Wei. "It is as though the Western powers are prepared to commence World War III if adequately provoked."

"I would say that is an accurate assessment," said Admiral Miao.

"Thank you for your report, admiral," said Wei. And with that, he hung up the phone.

There was but one more report to be received before they would have to call President Xi. That would come from the Ministry of Foreign Affairs' Vice-Minister, Le Yucheng. This entire exercise was not stacking up to generate a favorable report, and the responsibility for submitting it would fall on Foreign Minister Wang. Later that day, Wang received Le's phone call.

"Minister Wang," began Le, "I have done as you asked and had our diplomats assess the political trends in the countries of the European Union, Europe, and around the world. I regret to say that our leaders underestimated the influence of the President of the United States in influencing the political decisions. Moreover, he has changed the minds of opinion leaders from socialist to capitalist so that they may preserve or revive their nations' economies and maintain their positions of power over the citizenry whose political belief systems they embrace.

"The leader of the heads of state who still hold on to their capitalist principals without external influence remains Marine Le Pen in France. She is joined, most notably, by Boris Johnson of the United Kingdom. There are, of course, several others, but the impact of their countries on the continent's prosperity is negligible."

"But the influence of our propaganda in the EU's social media appeared to be having a significant impact on the temperament of the populace and driving the politics of their leaders to the Left," said Wang. "I had thought that we had moved nearly all of the European leaders' ideologies to the Left from where they started and that those moves had influenced their countries' populations. Do you mean to tell me that this Clint Anderson's words had such an overwhelming impact?"

"I'm afraid so, Minister Wang," said Le.

"Very well then," responded Wang. "If that is the current state of affairs, it is essential that I inform President Xi of just that. Neither our economic nor military status are in any way improved. It would be imprudent to continue our initiative in Europe if the apparent ends do not justify our current means."

It was late evening in Beijing, but Minister Wang felt compelled to call President Xi as soon as possible. He placed the call and waited to be connected. He patiently waited as the call, which had gone through Xi's office's switchboard, was finally routed to his residence. After President Xi came on the line, Minister Wang began.

The exchange between Wang and Xi could well have been a long and rambling dialogue, but that was not Xi's style. He had assigned his three ministers aboard the *Ford* three very specific tasks. The Minister of Commerce was to assess the impact of China's initiative on the world's economies. The Minister of National Defense was to determine the readiness postures of both China's military and its potential adversaries. And the Foreign Minister was to ascertain the tone of the political state of affairs abroad. All three had done their jobs admirably, and Minister Wang provided President Xi with their reports.

Xi listened attentively. His ire grew by the minute, but he did not interrupt. When Wang was finished, Xi thanked him for his report and told him to express his appreciation to the other ministers for their thoroughness. He then told Wang that he would have them contacted when he had reached his decision as to how he would proceed.

President Xi had a relatively simple choice to make. He could release Denmark from its commitments for port facilities and naval base and abandon the administration of the EU's 5G network. Or he could undertake the preparation of his nation for the prosecution of World War III.

Chapter Thirty-six

In the final analysis, President Xi had no choice whatsoever. While China's military capability *may* have been superior to that of any other single country with its hypersonic glide vehicles, new fleet of nuclear submarines, and other weapons of mass destruction, the aggregate power of the United States and NATO could not be overcome. The time for China to overwhelm the cumulative might of the remainder of its adversarial nations' forces had not yet come.

President Xi's first order of business was to place a phone call to President Anderson in Washington where it was approaching Noon. Anderson was interrupted during his lunch in the residence and told that Xi was on the phone. When he finally took the call, the exchange was curt and without emotion. Xi announced to him that he would capitulate to Anderson's demands and undertake the process in short order. He would leave it to Anderson to announce this decision to the various heads of state and the entire world. Before Xi hung up, he told Anderson that he trusted the United States would make arrangements to have his three captive ministers returned to Beijing. After the call, he ordered one of his deputies to call those ministers to inform them of his decision and their impending release.

The challenge for Xi now was how to tactfully withdraw from the current dilemma without bringing humiliation upon himself or disgrace on his country. Winning the bid to construct the 5G network in the European Union had brought about the engagement of China in the midst of the EU's political and economic affairs. The withdrawal from its politics and ideological affairs would simply mean gradually decreasing its presence on social media. Disengaging from its economy would be somewhat more complex.

The insinuation of Chinese companies into the consumer goods markets of the EU had been gradual and stealthy. Their withdrawal was, as with its politics, only a matter of a timely diminution in their presence on social media and in its economy. The most difficult and lengthiest phase of China's inserting itself into the day-to-day life of the residents of the European Union would be turning the operation of the 5G network, internet, and webcam interface infrastructure over to others to operate.

In order to accomplish this, China would start by soliciting from the contractors the initial list of corporate bidders. There were six principal cell phone manufacturers among the countries in the European Union. The four which had placed bids to construct its 5G network included Nokia from Finland, Ericsson from Sweden, Archos from France, and Blocc from Germany.

Nokia's proved to be the most competitive among the four. Consequently, it was agreed that they would pick up the management and ongoing implementation of the work which China had undertaken. Ironically, of course, Nokia no longer manufactured its cell phones and associated equipment in Finland. They were now all manufactured by Foxconn in China.

When the leaders of the EU learned this, they made it understood to the corporate heads of Nokia in Finland that it was their expectation that the manufacture of the equipment to be installed in Europe to replace that from Huawei and ZTE would be strictly overseen by Finnish engineers and computer scientists. Nokia concurred and the contract signed. Work would begin within 90 days.

Over that same 90-day period, any astute observer could deduce that the political and ideological content of the posts appearing on social media in the EU was more reflective of that of Europeans and less that of the Communist Chinese. The blatantly Chinese advertising for consumer goods diminished rapidly. And ads for those companies posing as European which were, in actuality, Chinese disappeared in a matter of weeks.

Within a week of the awarding of the 5G contract, the corporate leaders and chief electrical engineers from Nokia had been summoned to a meeting at the headquarters of the European Union in the office of the President of the EU, Ursula von der Leyen, in the Europa Building in Brussels. Also present were several heads of state including Mette

Frederiksen, the Prime Minister of Denmark, and Marine Le Pen, the President of France. Von der Leyen laid out the explicit expectations of the leaders of the EU to the delegation from Nokia.

The most important was that any critical components which China could have used to surveil Europe or may have been compromised would have to be replaced. Her explanation was simple. Several years earlier, a team of computer scientists from a Canadian computer security firm had determined that computer chips built for firms in Silicon Valley but manufactured by subcontractors in China had an extra semiconductor, not on the schematic plans given them, the size of a grain of rice which gave their manufacturer, and China, a back door into any network containing them. Those networks included those operated by Apple and Amazon Web Services (AWS). And AWS was utilized by several U.S. government agencies including the Central Intelligence Agency to handle highly classified documents and imagery.

The folks from Nokia got the message. They would have to carefully, and randomly, tear apart any network components built by Foxconn or any other Chinese company to ensure their integrity. That would add unanticipated costs to Nokia's work, but it was determined that they still wanted to retain the contract. The security of the European Union was at stake.

The Digital Silk Road

The EU could not simply shut down the 5G network or the internet. Both had become integral parts of daily life. And the webcam networks were one of the essential components of industry, be it commercial or military. They would just have to rebuild them one component at a time.

They started with the major server farms which enabled the network to operate and the switchers which directed the information to its designated destination. That began the process of rebuilding the network itself. But then there were the cell phones themselves. Having been built, for the most part, by Huawei and ZTE, each phone could potentially have implanted in it a clandestine chip which would allow it to be hacked or "bugged". And that phone could be carried by a government official or a captain of industry.

The EU set up a "trade-in" mechanism of sorts. It would take a cell phone in and give the trader a "clean" phone of similar value. They would then have Nokia scan the phone for potential bugs and place it on the second-hand market. There was a nominal financial loss in the transaction, but it could not be helped.

Over the coming months and years the European Union slowly but surely "purged" itself of the intrusive components introduced into its communications network and way of life by the Chinese. It had learned a hard lesson. You get what you pay for, and sometimes a great deal more.

There has always been war, and there always will be. Sometimes it is forestalled by what has been referred to as a "balance of terror". During the Cold War following World War II and lasting until the fall of the Soviet Union, there was a concept known as Mutually Assured Destruction, or MAD for short. A nuclear war initiated by either side would lead to the destruction of society on both sides. But a perceived imbalance of power can be relentlessly seductive to a potential aggressor.

Vietnam, a nation in Southeast Asia, was fought for by serial "liberators" for decades. In the 1960s and '70s, it was the United States. Notwithstanding the endless trail of armament and troops supporting Ho Chi Minh from North Vietnam and China, there was no doubt the Americans had both the weaponry and "know how" to win the war. But neither Kennedy nor McNamara, Johnson nor Nixon, had the political will to win. In the end, the Americans went home. Some in body bags. Some to go to college on the GI Bill. Some died of the effects of Agent Orange, the insidious herbicide and defoliant. And some broken.

War is a funny thing. Inevitably, the writers of history declare a winner. But neither the leaders nor the citizens of the nation deemed victorious have won anything.

The End

Made in the USA
Columbia, SC
27 March 2023

14358836R00138